DreamWorks CLASSICS PRESENTS

Shrek & Madagascar

MADAGASCAR STORIES!

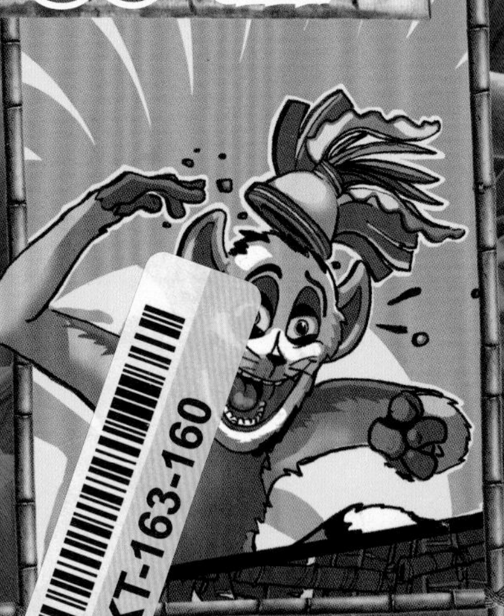

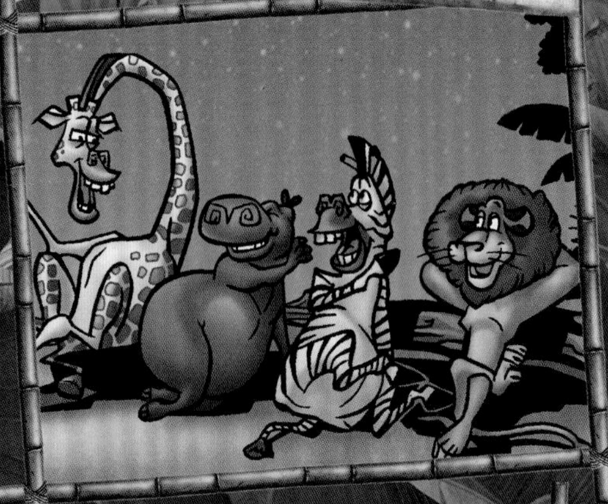

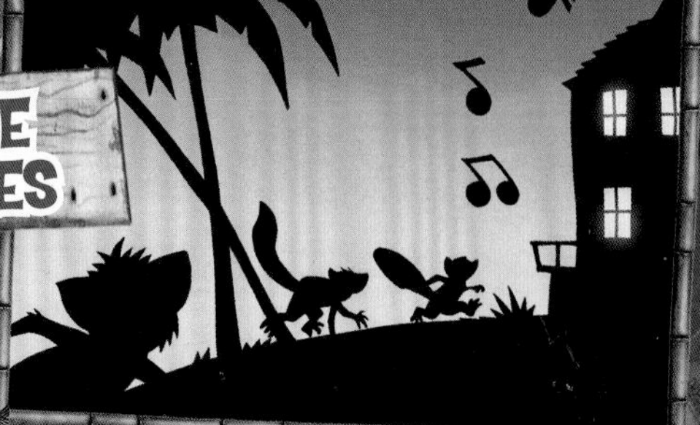

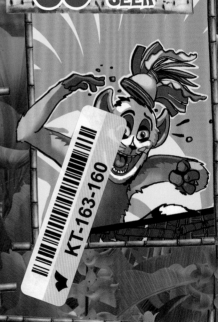

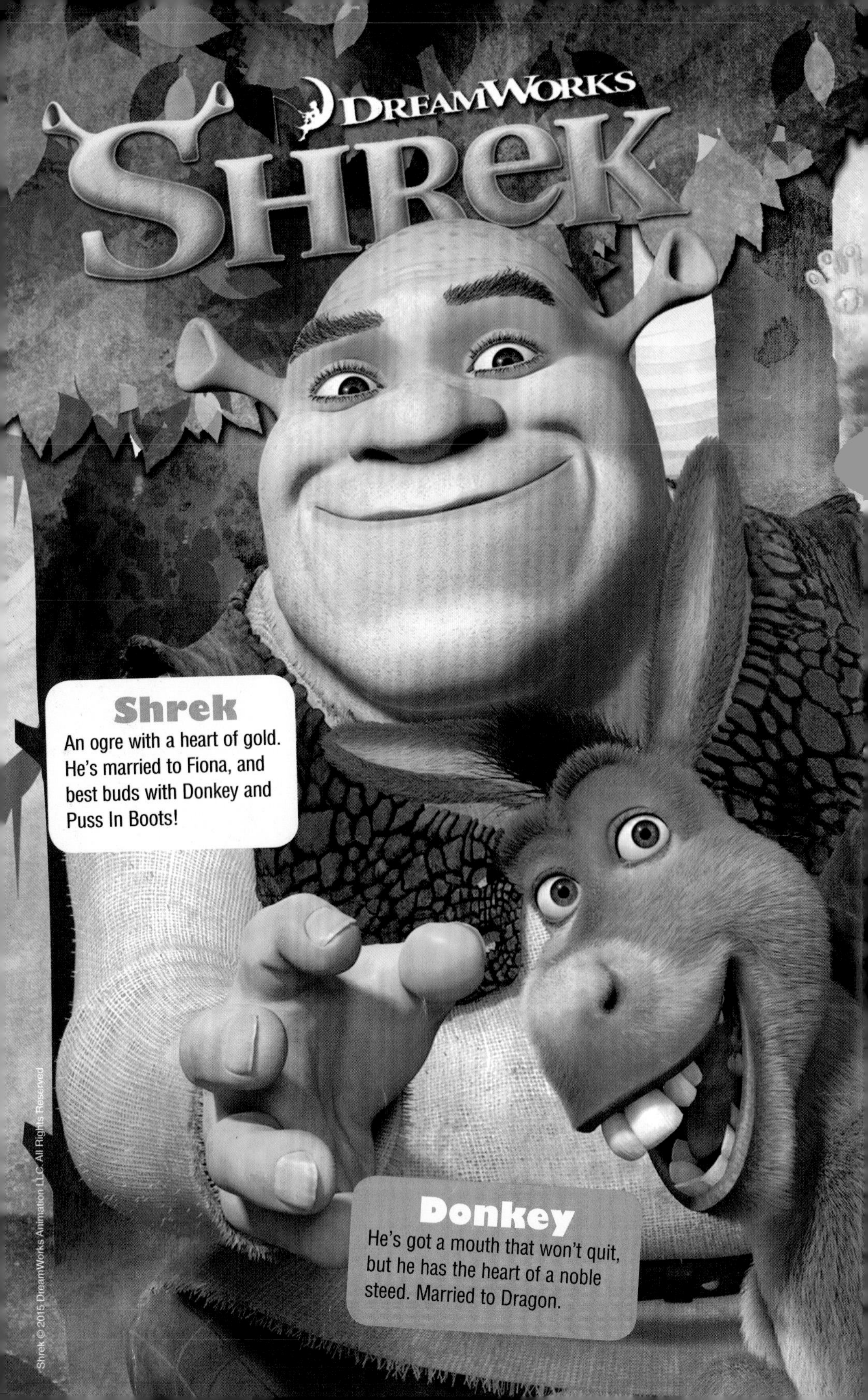
DreamWorks
Shrek
Shrek
An ogre with a heart of gold. He's married to Fiona, and best buds with Donkey and Puss In Boots!
Donkey
He's got a mouth that won't quit, but he has the heart of a noble steed. Married to Dragon.

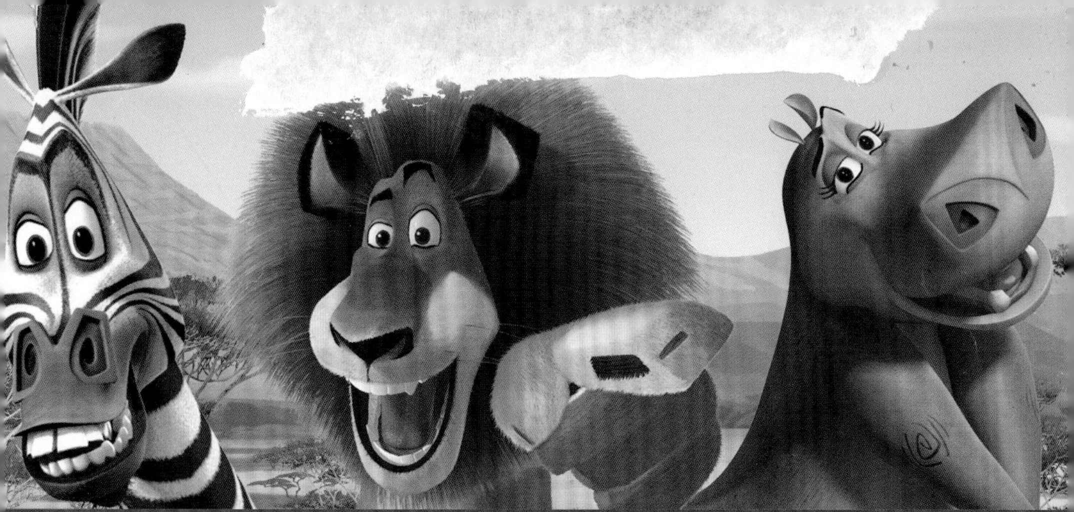

DREAMWORKS CLASSICS PRESENTS

SHREK & MADAGASCAR

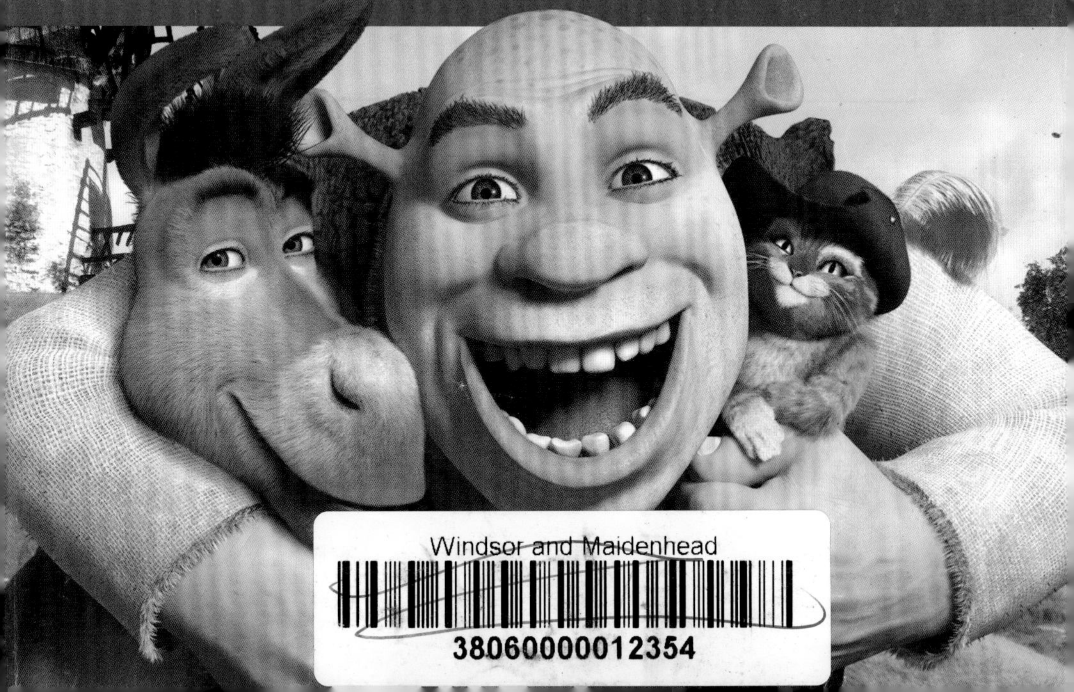

CONTENTS

SHREK COMICS!

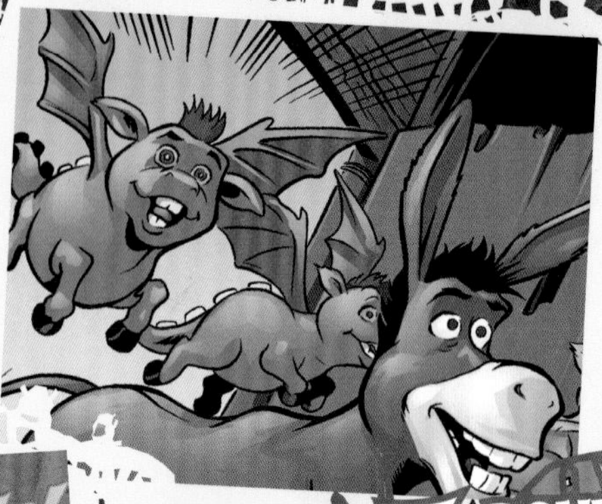

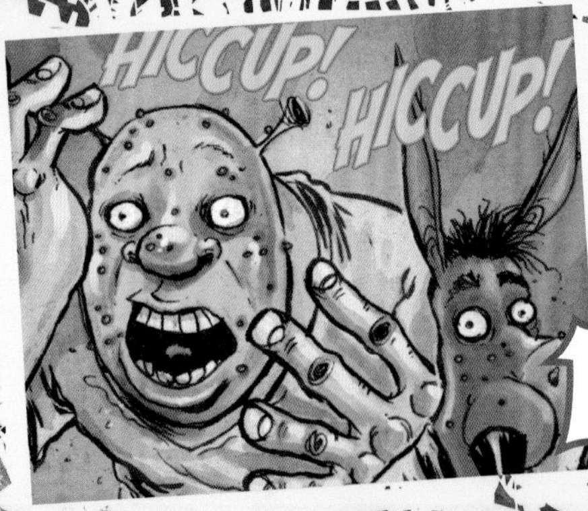
HICCUP!
HICCUP!

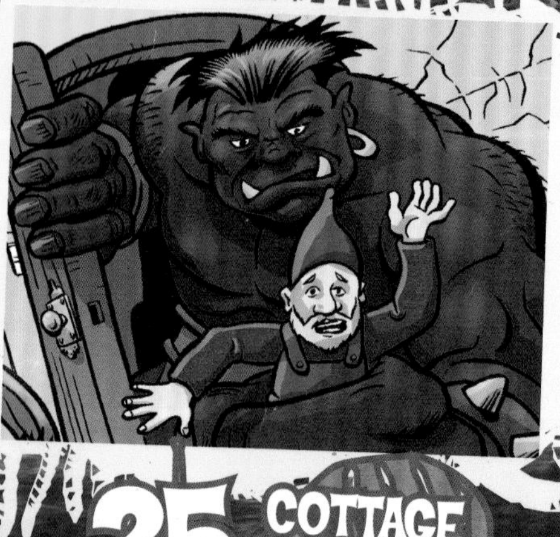

TITAN EDITORIAL
SENIOR EDITOR Martin Eden
PRODUCTION MANAGER Obi Onoura
PRODUCTION SUPERVISORS Maria James, Jackie Flook
PRODUCTION ASSISTANT Peter James
STUDIO MANAGER Selina Juneja
SENIOR SALES MANAGER Steve Tothill
MARKETING MANAGER Ricky Claydon
PUBLISHING MANAGER Darryl Tothill
PUBLISHING DIRECTOR Chris Teather
OPERATIONS DIRECTOR Leigh Baulch
EXECUTIVE DIRECTOR Vivian Cheung
PUBLISHER Nick Landau

ISBN: 9781782762461

Published by Titan Comics, a division of Titan Publishing Group Ltd. 144 Southwark St. London, SE1 0UP.

10 9 8 7 6 5 4 3 2 1

First printed in China in September 2015. A CIP catalogue record for this title is available from the British Library. Titan Comics. TC01552

Special thanks to Andrew James, Steve White and Donna Askem.

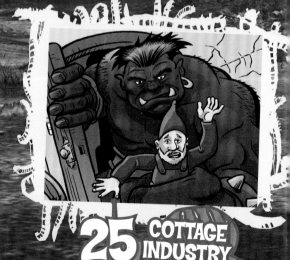

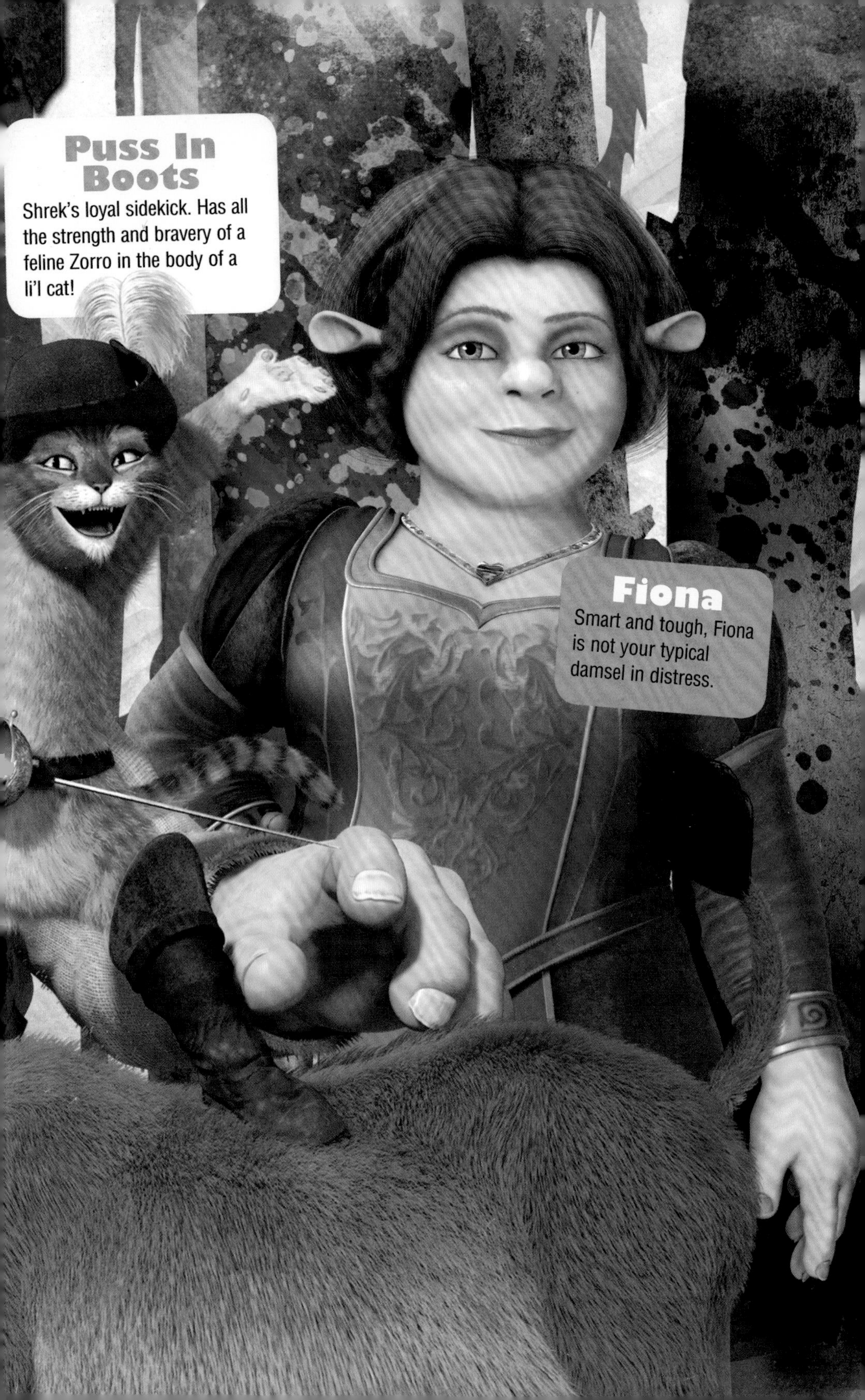
Puss In Boots
Shrek's loyal sidekick. Has all the strength and bravery of a feline Zorro in the body of a li'l cat!
Fiona
Smart and tough, Fiona is not your typical damsel in distress.

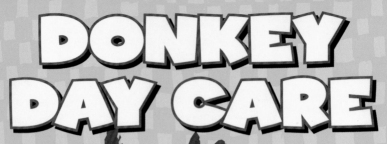

DONKEY DAY CARE

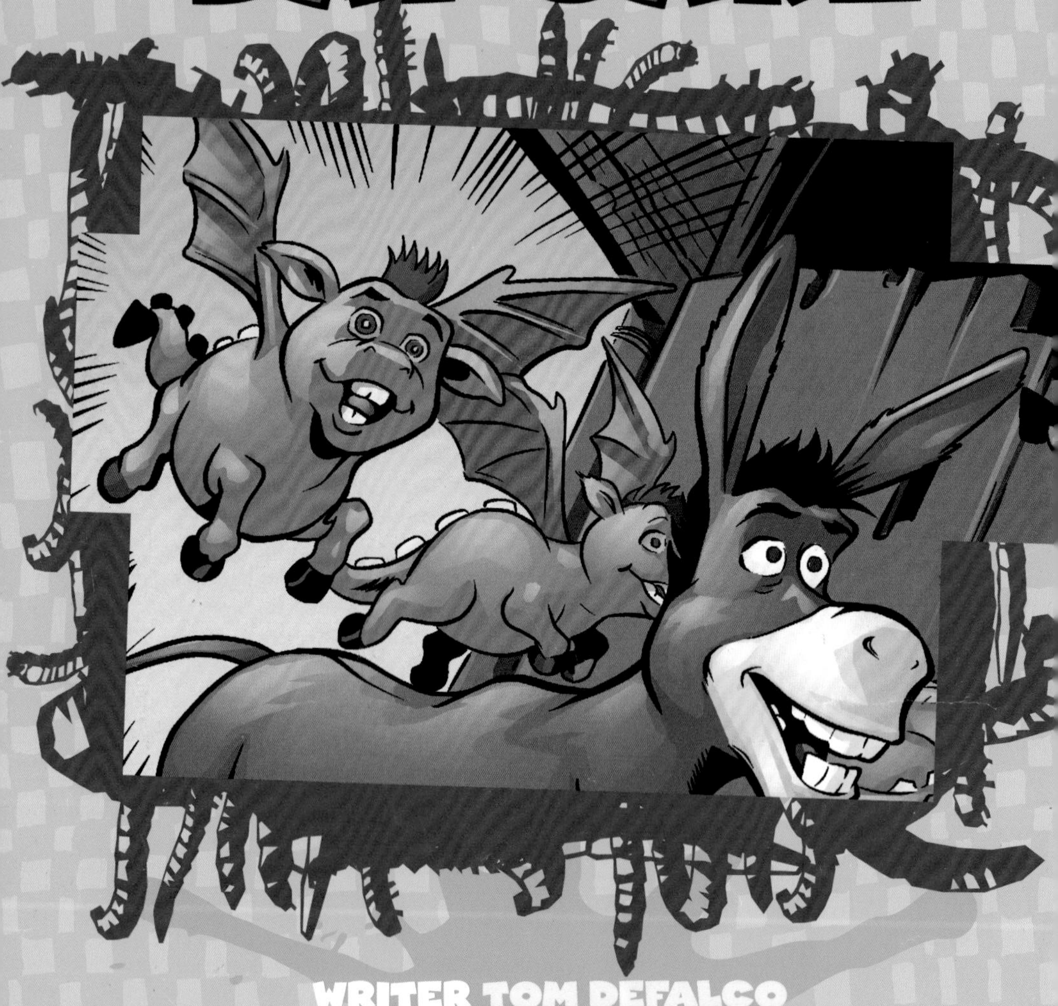

WRITER TOM DEFALCO
PENCILS SL GALLANT
INKS DAN DAVIS
COLORS HI-FI DESIGN
LETTERS JIMMY BETANCOURT/COMICRAFT

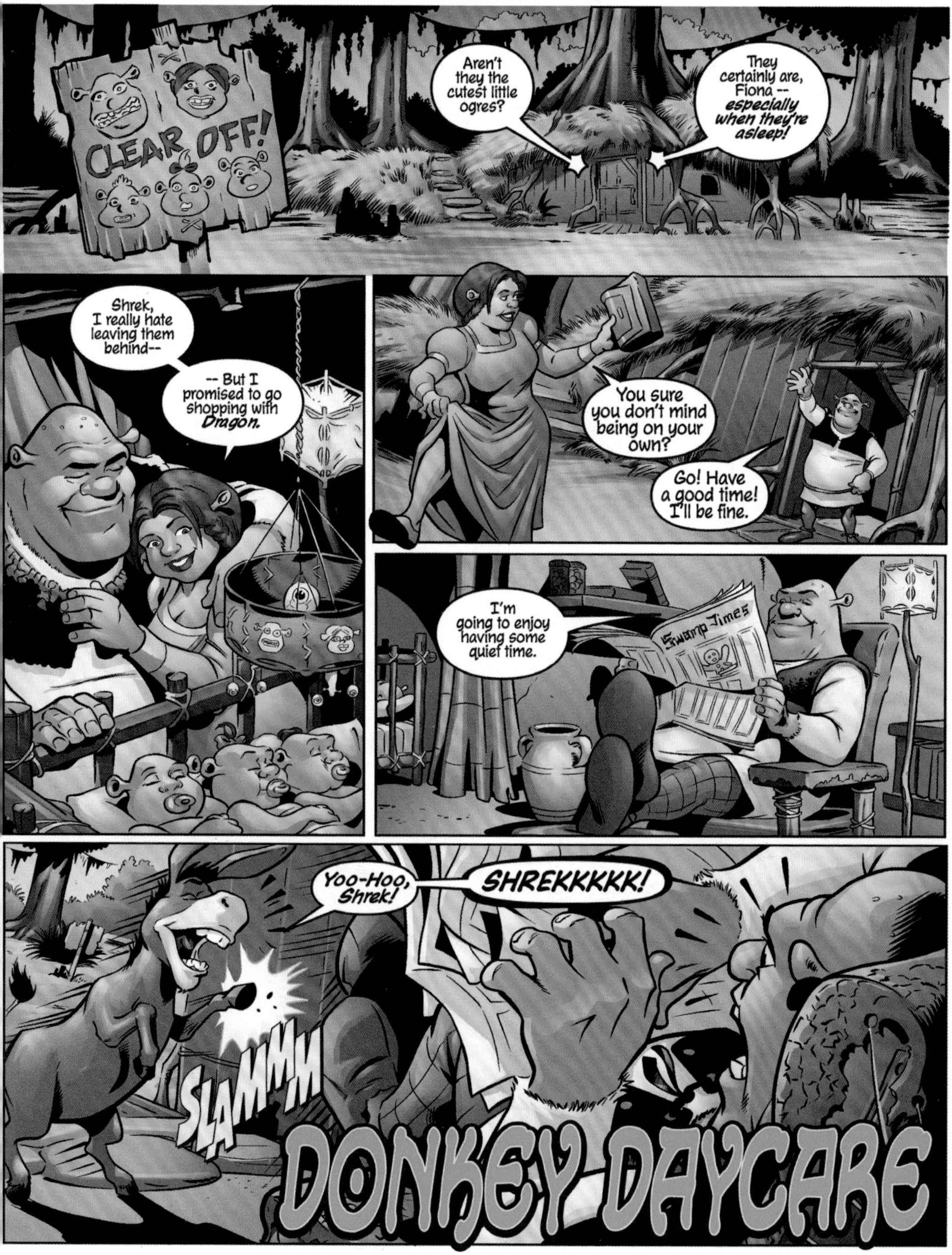
CLEAR OFF!
Aren't they the cutest little ogres?
They certainly are, Fiona -- *especially when they're asleep!*
Shrek, I really hate leaving them behind--
-- But I promised to go shopping with *Dragon.*
You sure you don't mind being on your own?
Go! Have a good time! I'll be fine.
Swamp Times
I'm going to enjoy having some quiet time.
Yoo-Hoo, Shrek!
SHREKKKKK!
SLAMMM
DONKEY DAYCARE

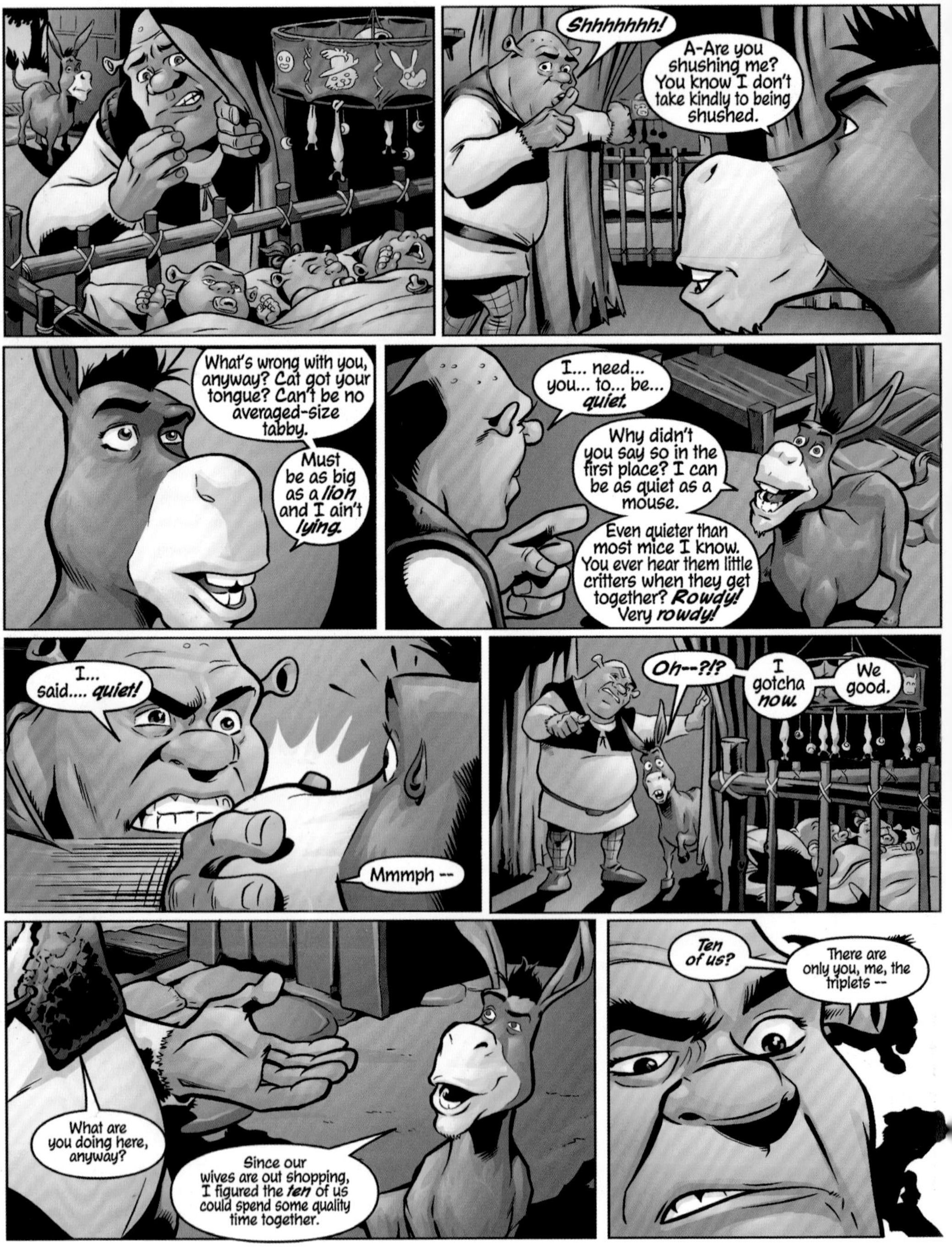
Shhhhhhh!
A-Are you shushing me? You know I don't take kindly to being shushed.
What's wrong with you, anyway? Cat got your tongue? Can't be no averaged-size tabby.
Must be as big as a lion and I ain't lying.
I... need... you... to... be... quiet.
Why didn't you say so in the first place? I can be as quiet as a mouse.
Even quieter than most mice I know. You ever hear them little critters when they get together? Rowdy! Very rowdy!
I... said.... quiet!
Mmmph --
Oh--?!?
I gotcha now.
We good.
What are you doing here, anyway?
Since our wives are out shopping, I figured the ten of us could spend some quality time together.
Ten of us?
There are only you, me, the triplets --

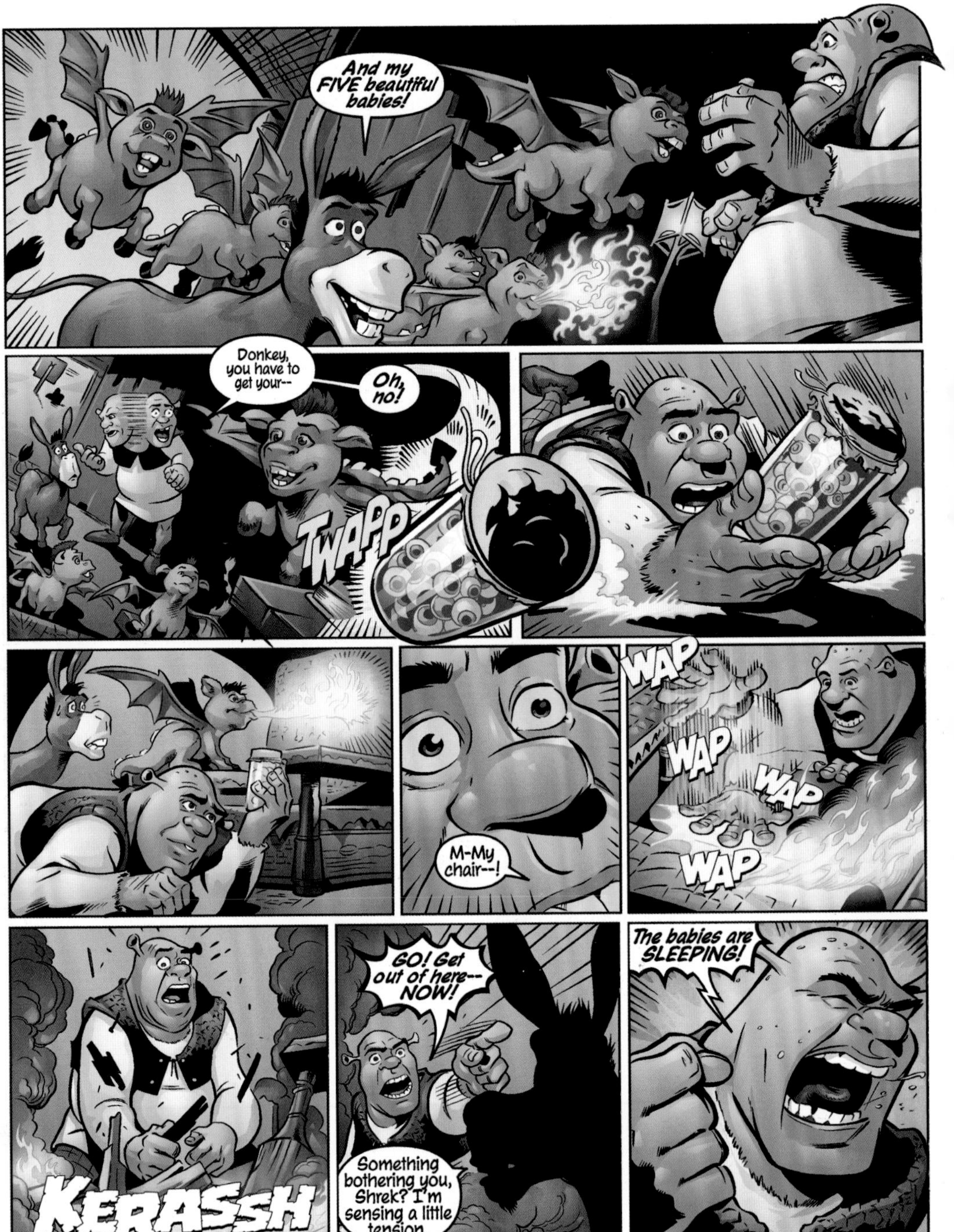
And my FIVE beautiful babies!
Donkey, you have to get your--
Oh, no!
TWAPP
M-My chair--!
WAP
WAP
WAP
WAP
KERASSH
GO! Get out of here-- NOW!
Something bothering you, Shrek? I'm sensing a little tension.
The babies are SLEEPING!

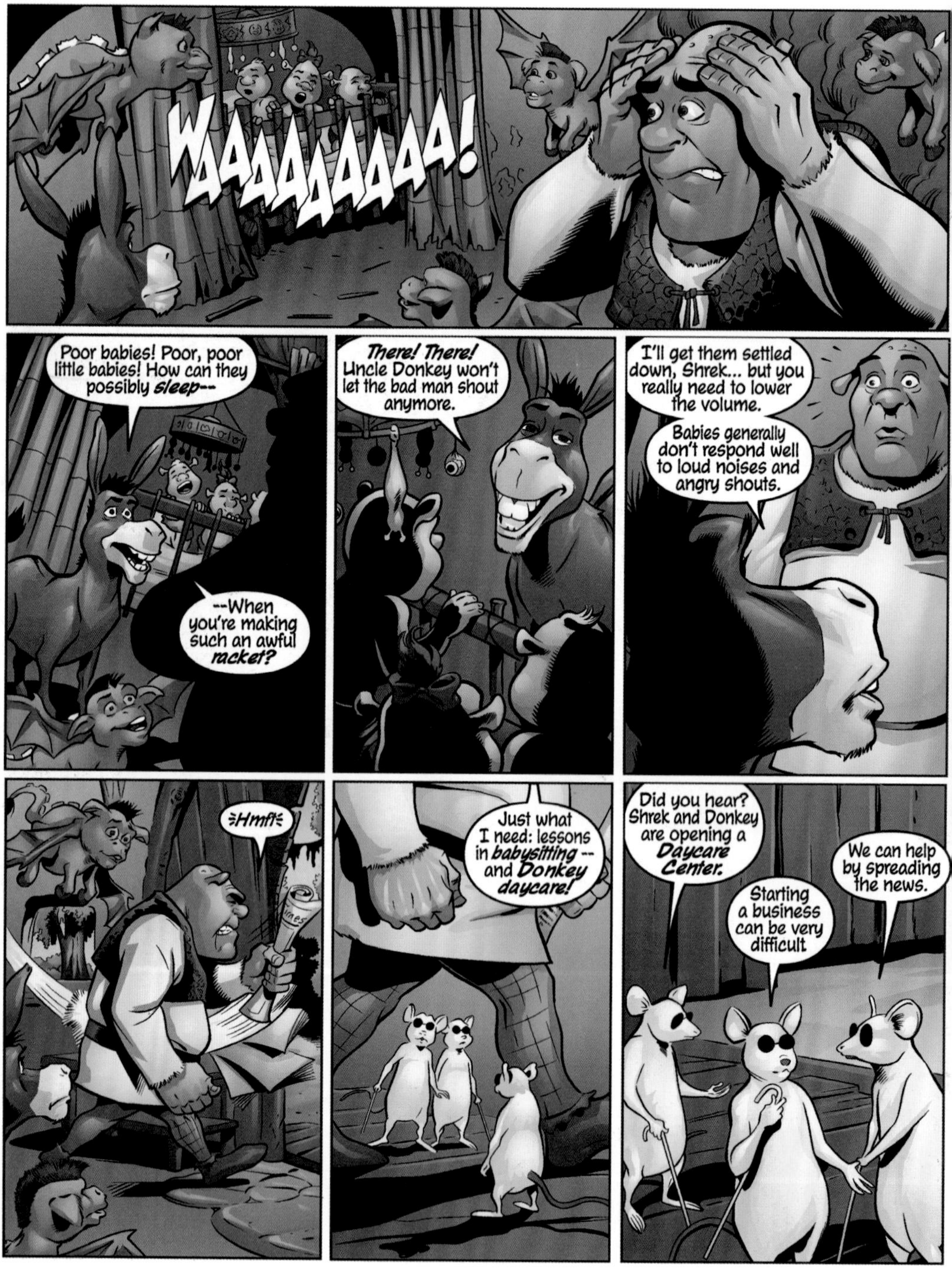
WAAAAAAAAA!
Poor babies! Poor, poor little babies! How can they possibly *sleep*--
--When you're making such an awful *racket?*
There! There! Uncle Donkey won't let the bad man shout anymore.
I'll get them settled down, Shrek... but you really need to lower the volume.
Babies generally don't respond well to loud noises and angry shouts.
Hmf!
Just what I need: lessons in *babysitting* -- and *Donkey daycare!*
Did you hear? Shrek and Donkey are opening a *Daycare Center.*
Starting a business can be very difficult
We can help by spreading the news.

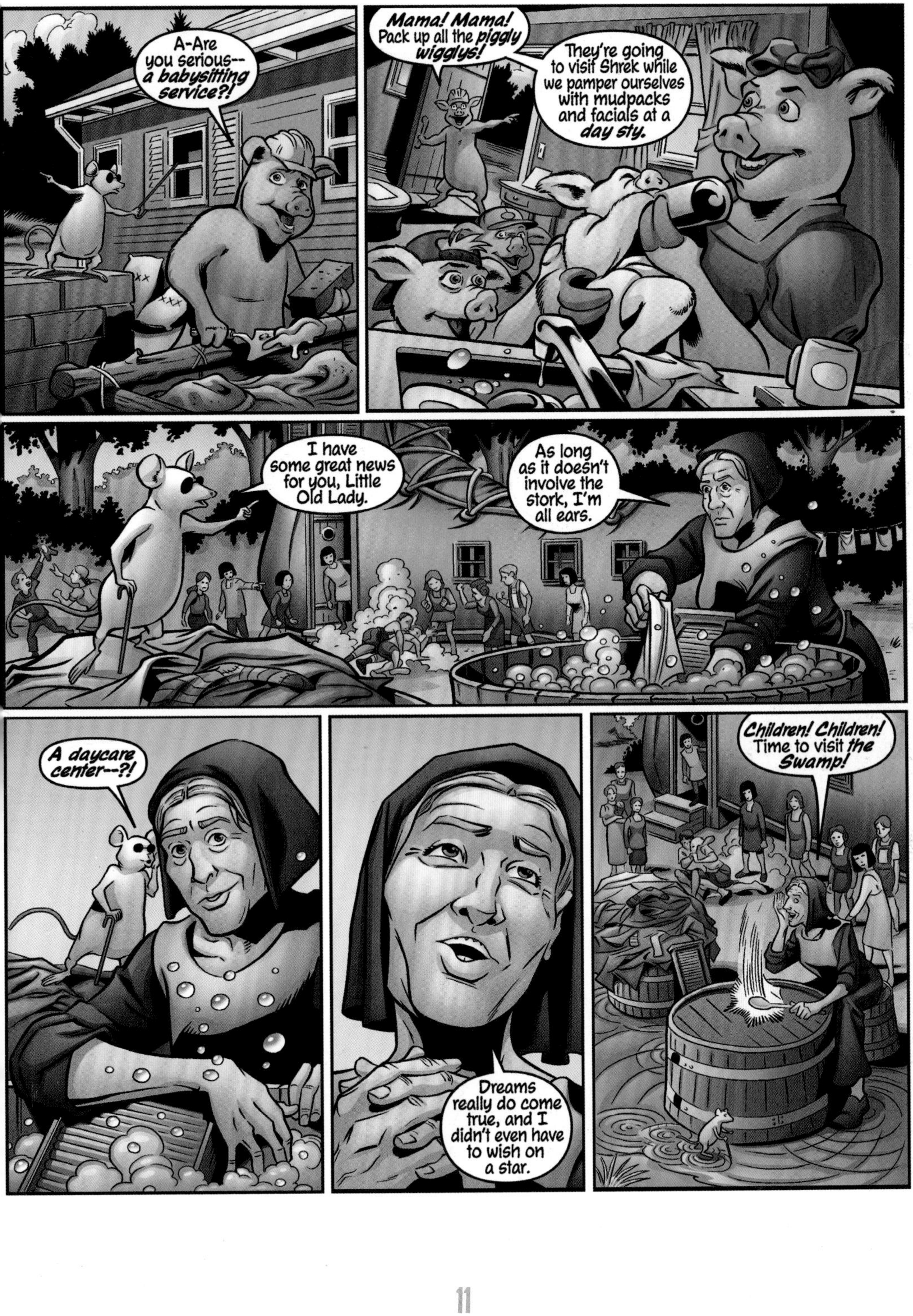
A-Are you serious-- a babysitting service?!
Mama! Mama! Pack up all the piggly wigglys!
They're going to visit Shrek while we pamper ourselves with mudpacks and facials at a day sty.
I have some great news for you, Little Old Lady.
As long as it doesn't involve the stork, I'm all ears.
A daycare center--?!
Dreams really do come true, and I didn't even have to wish on a star.
Children! Children! Time to visit the Swamp!

Ahhhhhhhh!
I feel better now.
All I really needed was a few minutes of peace and--
-- Quiet?!
Donkey--!
Are we back to *shouting*?
I thought we agreed to use an *indoor* voice.
W-Where'd all these *children* come from?

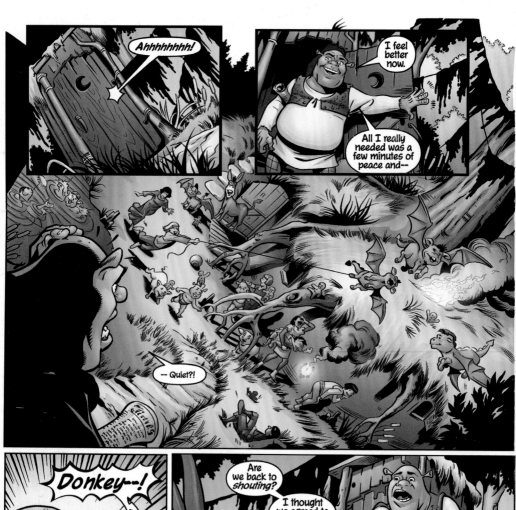

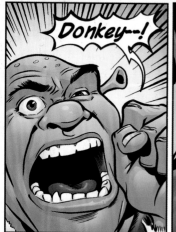

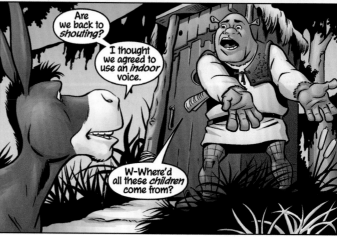

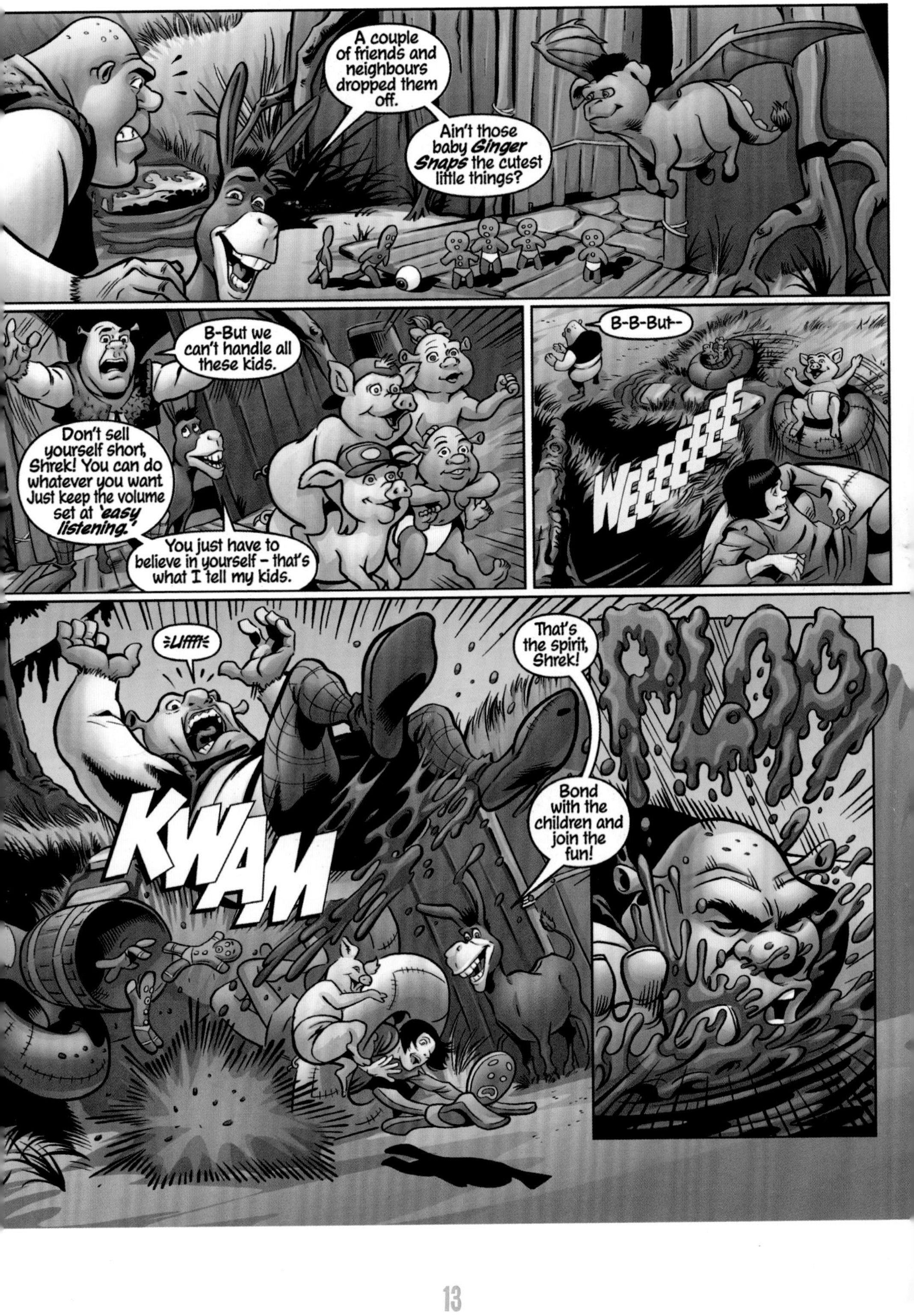
A couple of friends and neighbours dropped them off.
Ain't those baby Ginger Snaps the cutest little things?
B-But we can't handle all these kids.
Don't sell yourself short, Shrek! You can do whatever you want Just keep the volume set at 'easy listening.'
You just have to believe in yourself – that's what I tell my kids.
B-B-But–
WEEEEEEEE
Ufff!
KWAM
That's the spirit, Shrek!
Bond with the children and join the fun!
PLOP

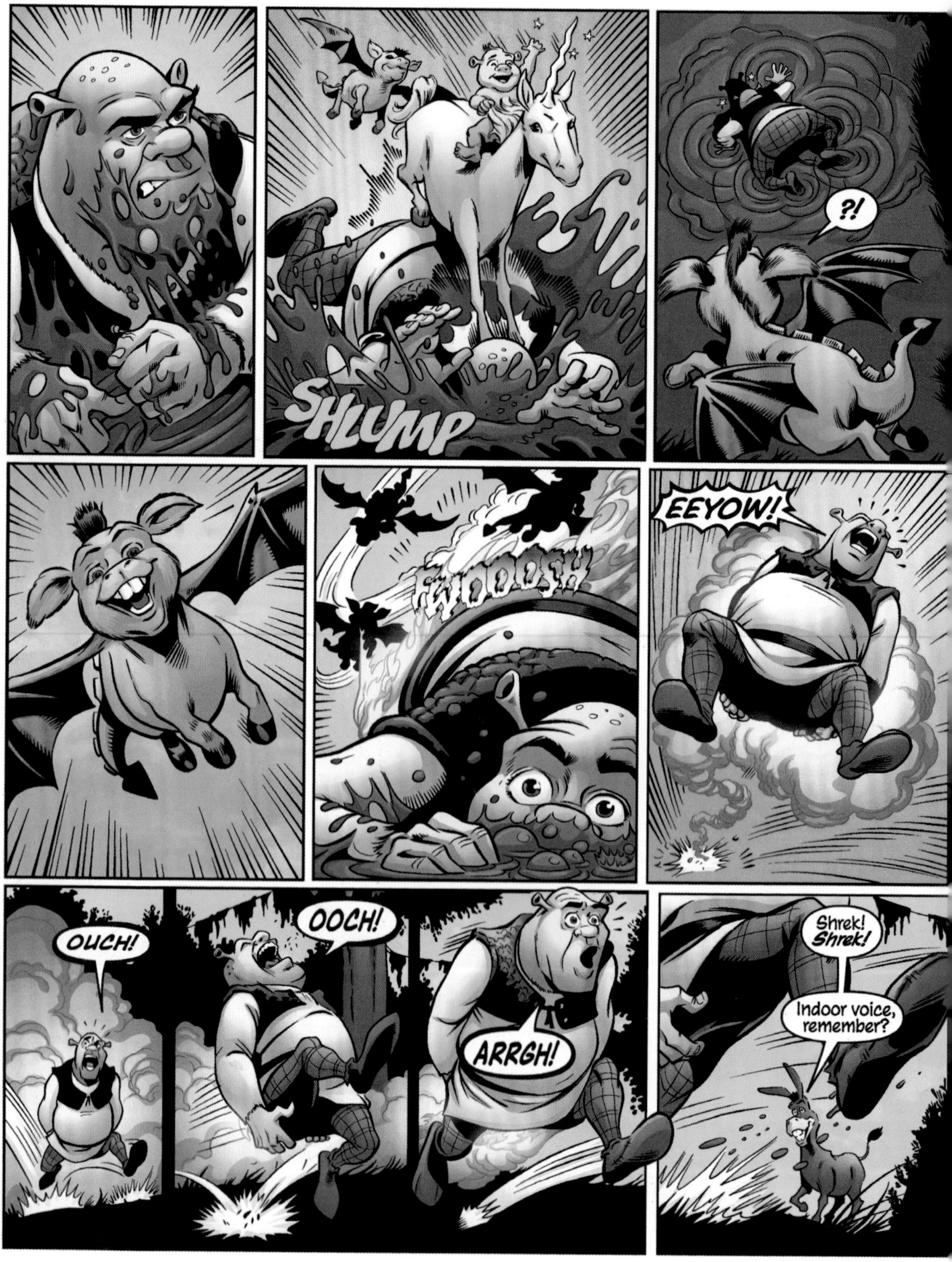
SHLUMP
?!
FWOOOSH
EEYOW!
OUCH!
OOCH!
ARRGH!
Shrek! Shrek!
Indoor voice, remember?

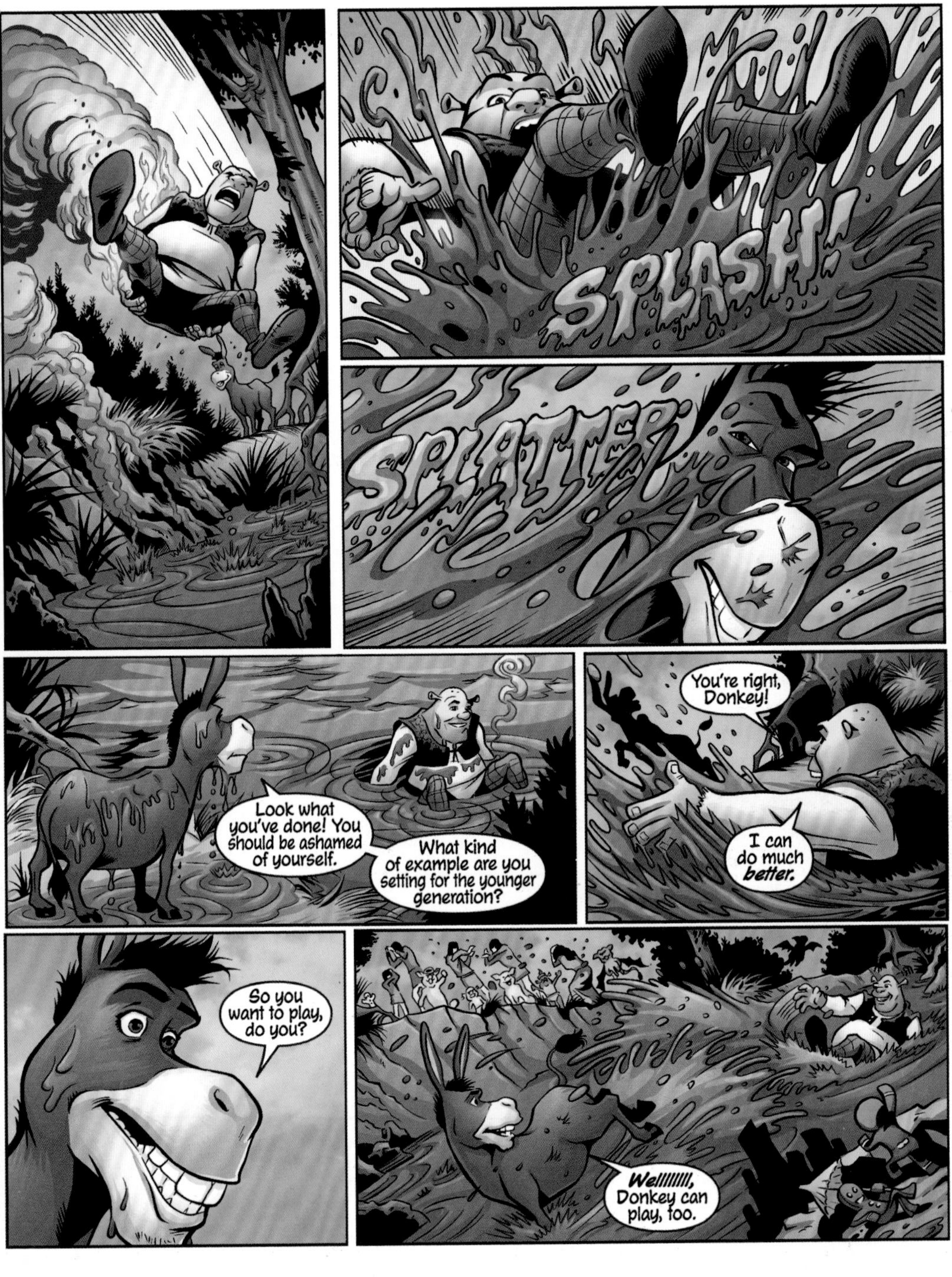
SPLASH!
SPLATTER
Look what you've done! You should be ashamed of yourself.
What kind of example are you setting for the younger generation?
You're right, Donkey!
I can do much *better.*
So you want to play, do you?
Wellllllll, Donkey can play, too.

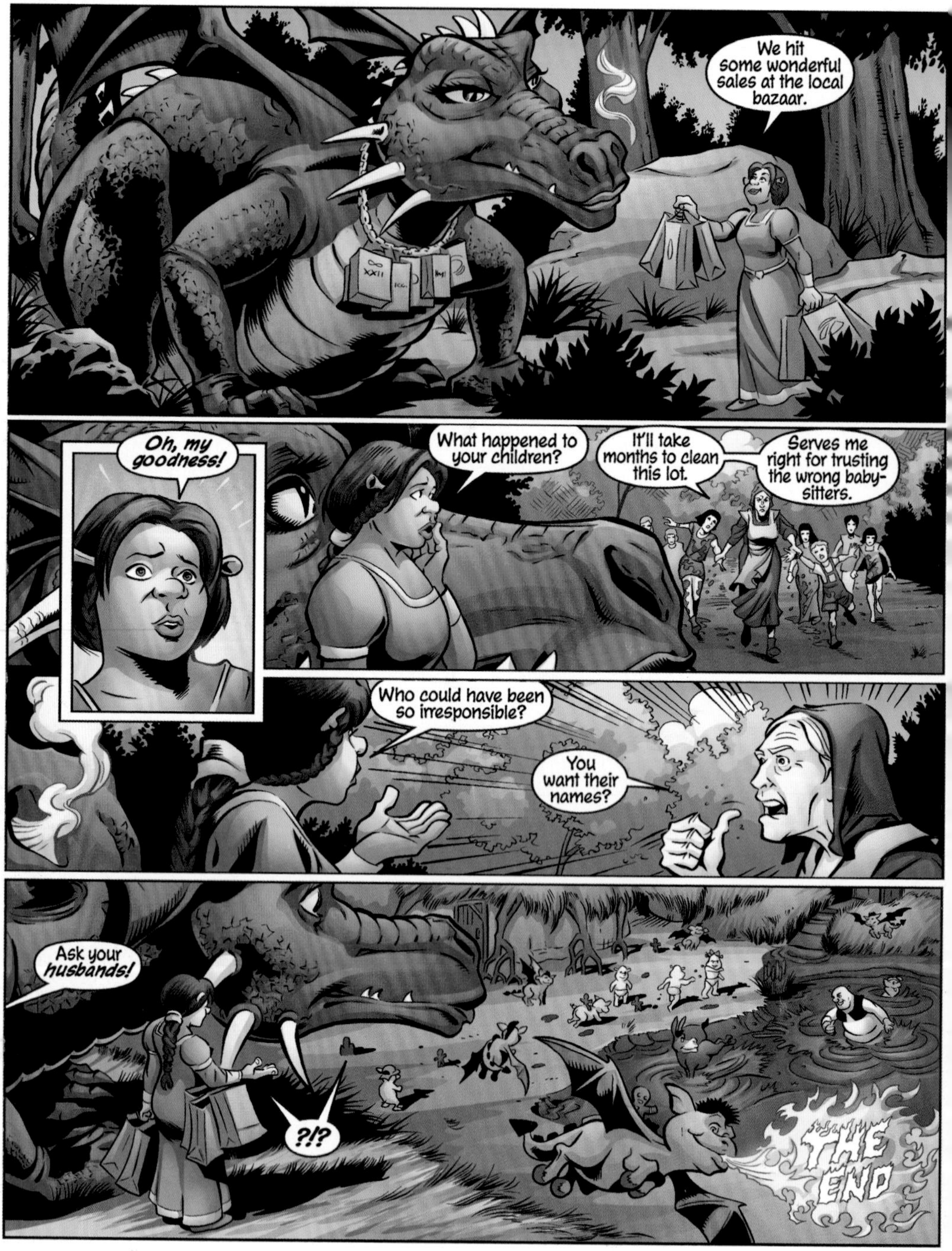
We hit some wonderful sales at the local bazaar.
Oh, my goodness!
What happened to your children?
It'll take months to clean this lot.
Serves me right for trusting the wrong baby-sitters.
Who could have been so irresponsible?
You want their names?
Ask your husbands!
?!?
THE END

FAIRY BERRY FEVER

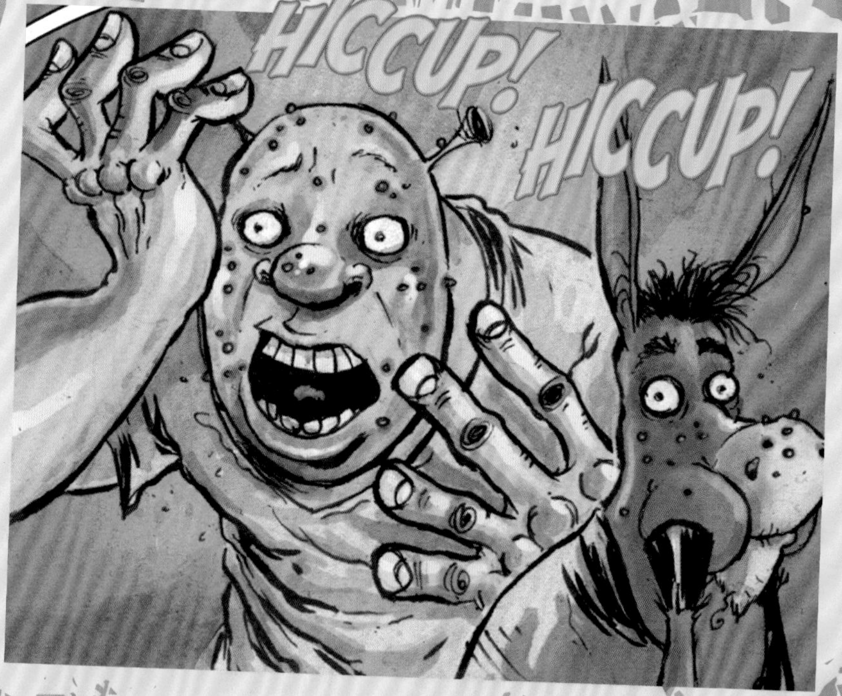
HICCUP!
HICCUP!

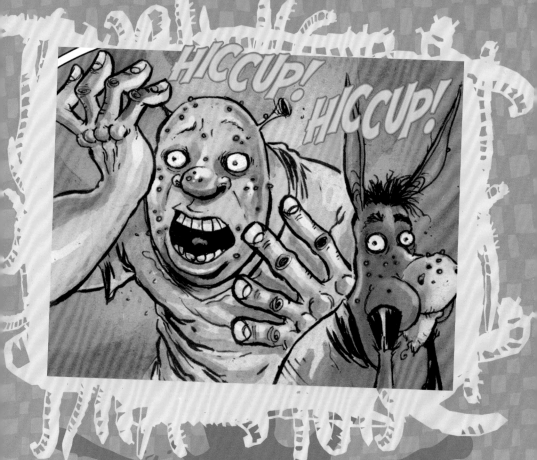

WRITER KEVIN FREEMAN
ART DREW RAUSCH
COLORS MATT KAUFENBERG
LETTERS CHRIS STUDBAKER

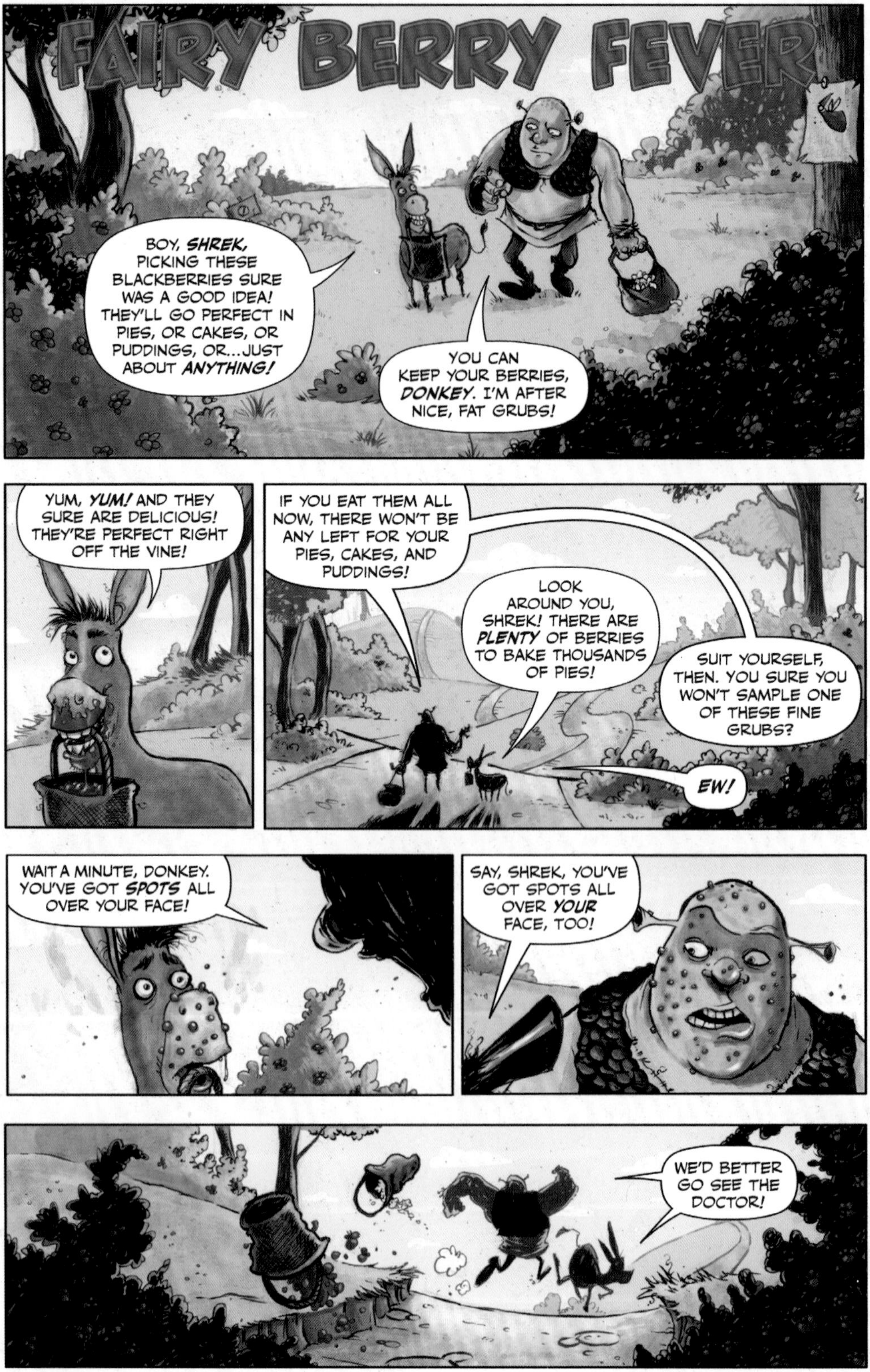

FAIRY BERRY FEVER
BOY, SHREK, PICKING THESE BLACKBERRIES SURE WAS A GOOD IDEA! THEY'LL GO PERFECT IN PIES, OR CAKES, OR PUDDINGS, OR...JUST ABOUT ANYTHING!
YOU CAN KEEP YOUR BERRIES, DONKEY. I'M AFTER NICE, FAT GRUBS!
YUM, YUM! AND THEY SURE ARE DELICIOUS! THEY'RE PERFECT RIGHT OFF THE VINE!
IF YOU EAT THEM ALL NOW, THERE WON'T BE ANY LEFT FOR YOUR PIES, CAKES, AND PUDDINGS!
LOOK AROUND YOU, SHREK! THERE ARE PLENTY OF BERRIES TO BAKE THOUSANDS OF PIES!
SUIT YOURSELF, THEN. YOU SURE YOU WON'T SAMPLE ONE OF THESE FINE GRUBS?
EW!
WAIT A MINUTE, DONKEY. YOU'VE GOT SPOTS ALL OVER YOUR FACE!
SAY, SHREK, YOU'VE GOT SPOTS ALL OVER YOUR FACE, TOO!
WE'D BETTER GO SEE THE DOCTOR!

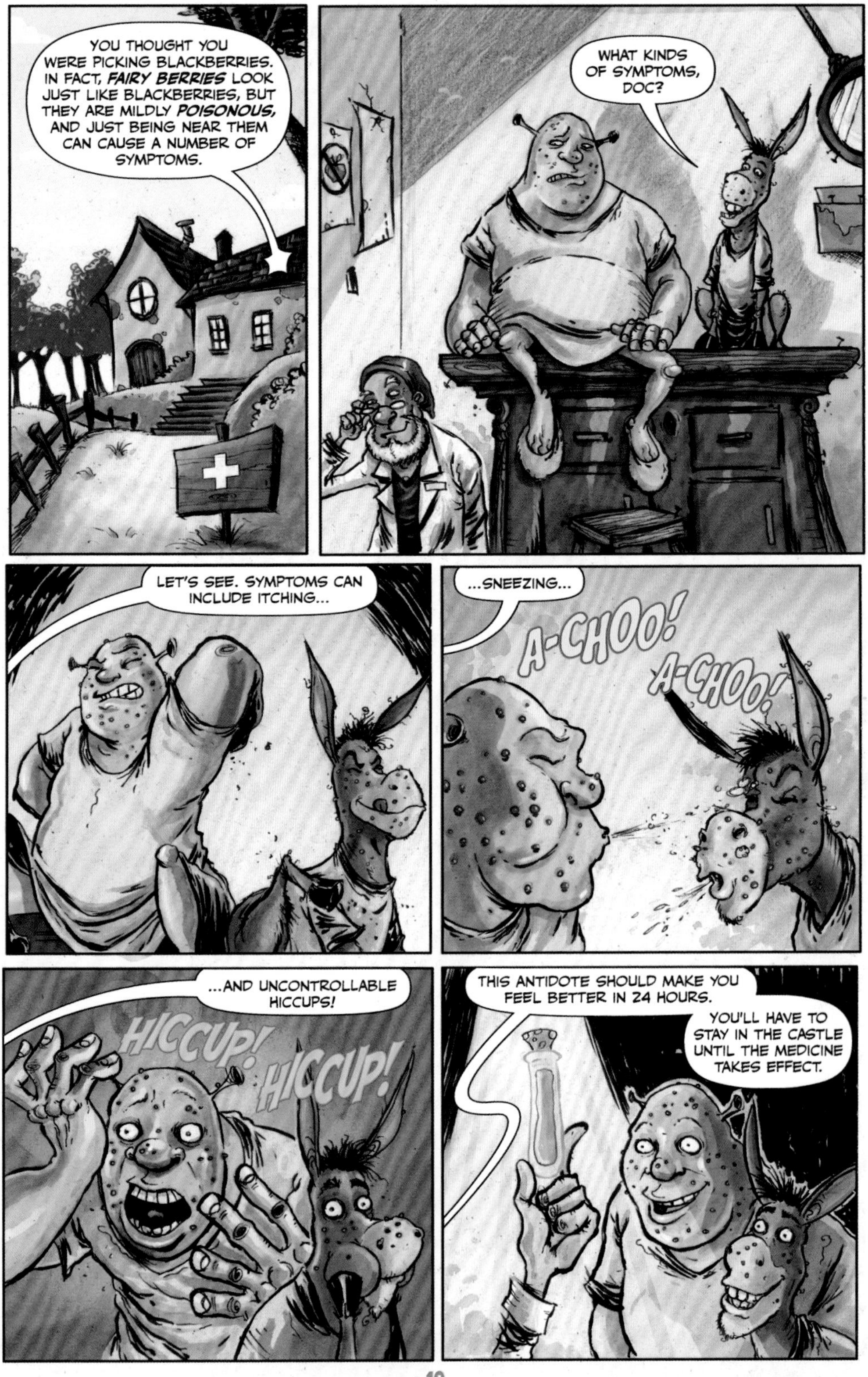
YOU THOUGHT YOU WERE PICKING BLACKBERRIES. IN FACT, FAIRY BERRIES LOOK JUST LIKE BLACKBERRIES, BUT THEY ARE MILDLY POISONOUS, AND JUST BEING NEAR THEM CAN CAUSE A NUMBER OF SYMPTOMS.
WHAT KINDS OF SYMPTOMS, DOC?
LET'S SEE. SYMPTOMS CAN INCLUDE ITCHING...
...SNEEZING...
A-CHOO!
A-CHOO!
...AND UNCONTROLLABLE HICCUPS!
HICCUP!
HICCUP!
THIS ANTIDOTE SHOULD MAKE YOU FEEL BETTER IN 24 HOURS.
YOU'LL HAVE TO STAY IN THE CASTLE UNTIL THE MEDICINE TAKES EFFECT.

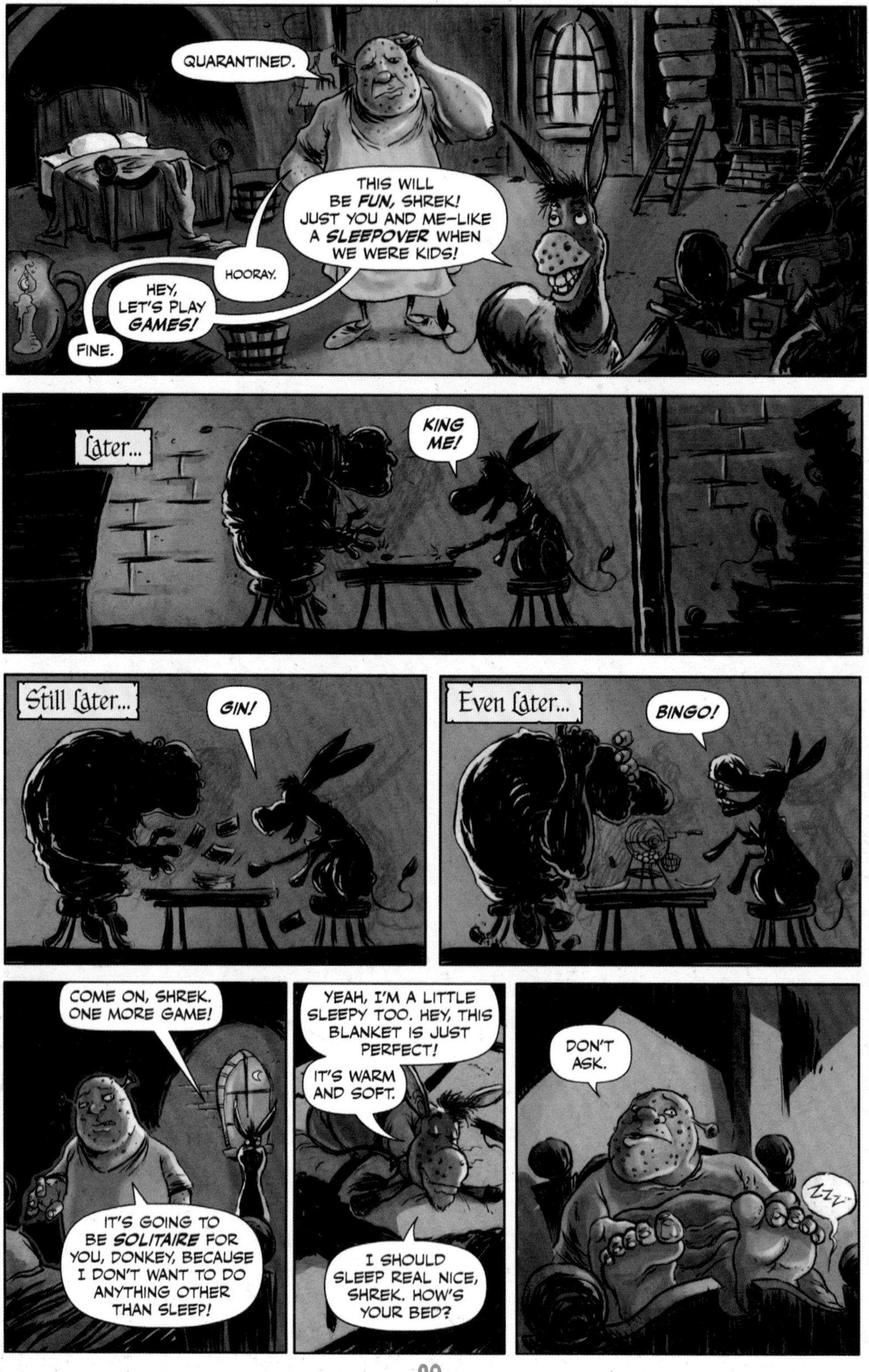
QUARANTINED.
THIS WILL BE *FUN,* SHREK! JUST YOU AND ME—LIKE A *SLEEPOVER* WHEN WE WERE KIDS!
HOORAY.
HEY, LET'S PLAY *GAMES!*
FINE.
Later...
KING ME!
Still Later...
GIN!
Even Later...
BINGO!
COME ON, SHREK. ONE MORE GAME!
IT'S GOING TO BE *SOLITAIRE* FOR YOU, DONKEY, BECAUSE I DON'T WANT TO DO ANYTHING OTHER THAN SLEEP!
YEAH, I'M A LITTLE SLEEPY TOO. HEY, THIS BLANKET IS JUST PERFECT!
IT'S WARM AND SOFT.
I SHOULD SLEEP REAL NICE, SHREK. HOW'S YOUR BED?
DON'T ASK.
ZZZ

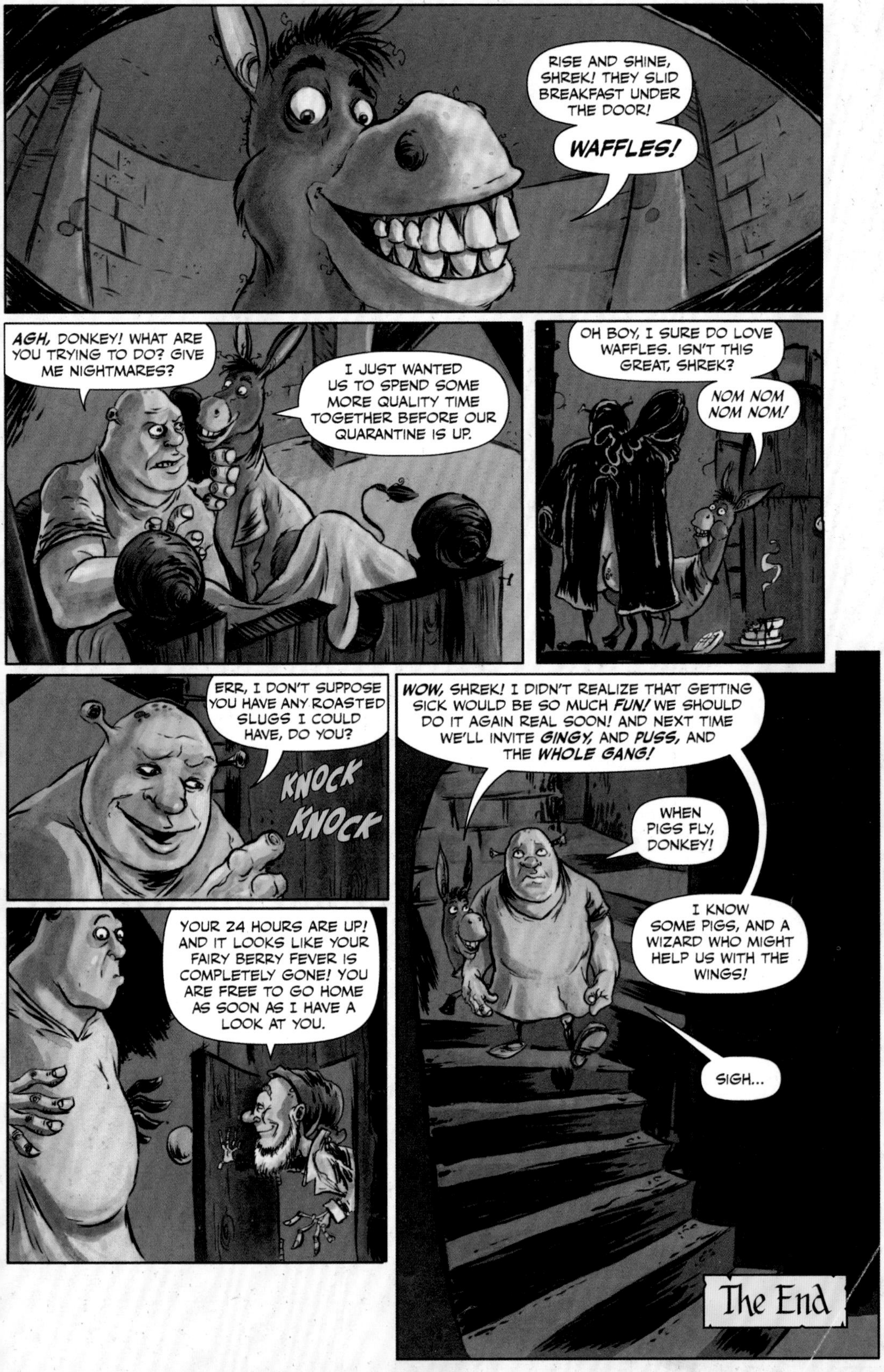
RISE AND SHINE, SHREK! THEY SLID BREAKFAST UNDER THE DOOR!
WAFFLES!
AGH, DONKEY! WHAT ARE YOU TRYING TO DO? GIVE ME NIGHTMARES?
I JUST WANTED US TO SPEND SOME MORE QUALITY TIME TOGETHER BEFORE OUR QUARANTINE IS UP.
OH BOY, I SURE DO LOVE WAFFLES. ISN'T THIS GREAT, SHREK?
NOM NOM NOM NOM!
ERR, I DON'T SUPPOSE YOU HAVE ANY ROASTED SLUGS I COULD HAVE, DO YOU?
KNOCK KNOCK
YOUR 24 HOURS ARE UP! AND IT LOOKS LIKE YOUR FAIRY BERRY FEVER IS COMPLETELY GONE! YOU ARE FREE TO GO HOME AS SOON AS I HAVE A LOOK AT YOU.
WOW, SHREK! I DIDN'T REALIZE THAT GETTING SICK WOULD BE SO MUCH FUN! WE SHOULD DO IT AGAIN REAL SOON! AND NEXT TIME WE'LL INVITE GINGY, AND PUSS, AND THE WHOLE GANG!
WHEN PIGS FLY, DONKEY!
I KNOW SOME PIGS, AND A WIZARD WHO MIGHT HELP US WITH THE WINGS!
SIGH...
The End

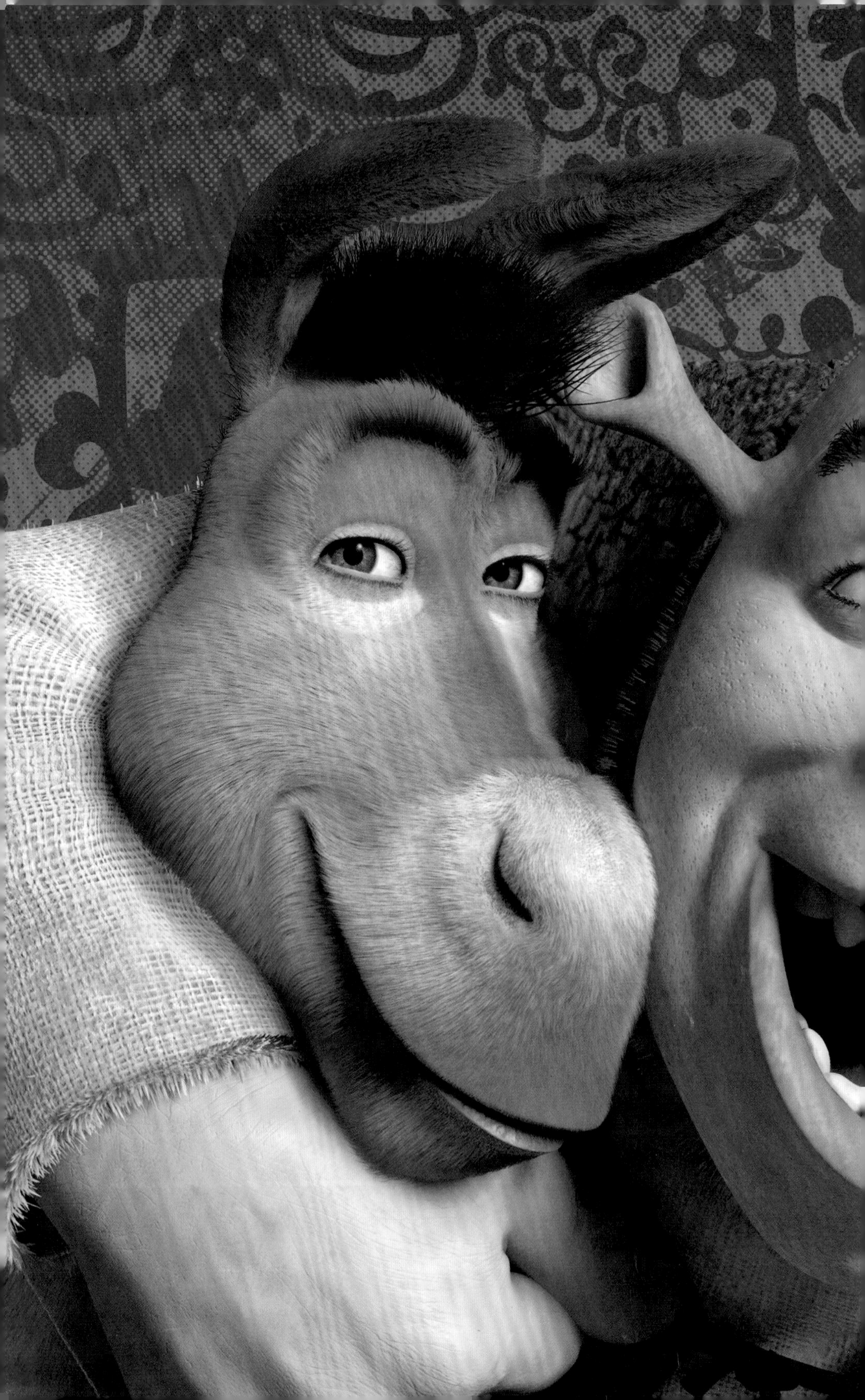

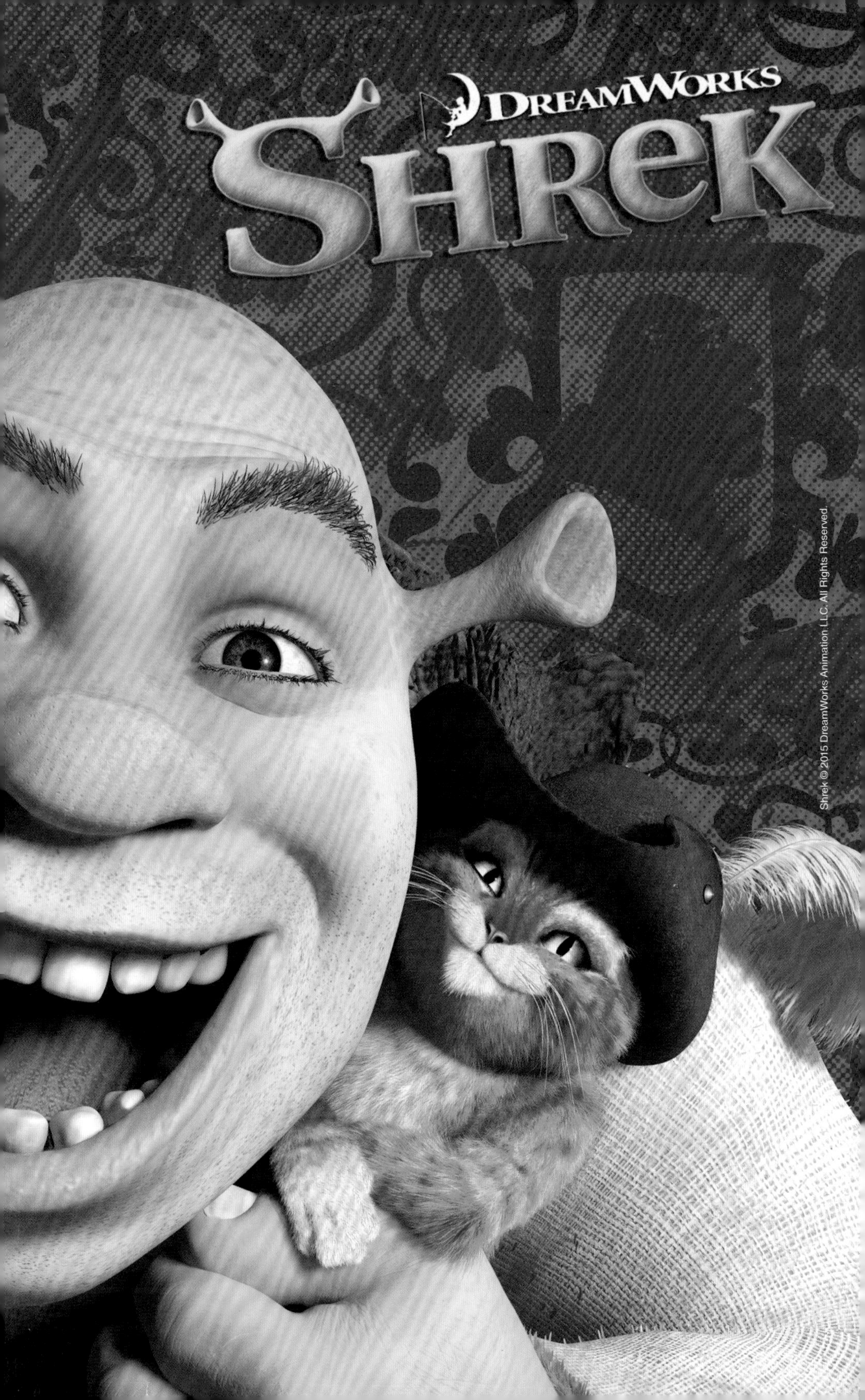
DreamWorks
Shrek

WARDROBE WRONG-DOING

WRITERS DAN ABNETT & ANDY LANNING
PENCILS BRIAN WILLIAMSON
INKS BAMBOS GEORGIOU
COLORS WILDIDEAS
LETTERS JIMMY BETANCOURT/COMICRAFT

WARDROBE WRONG-DOING

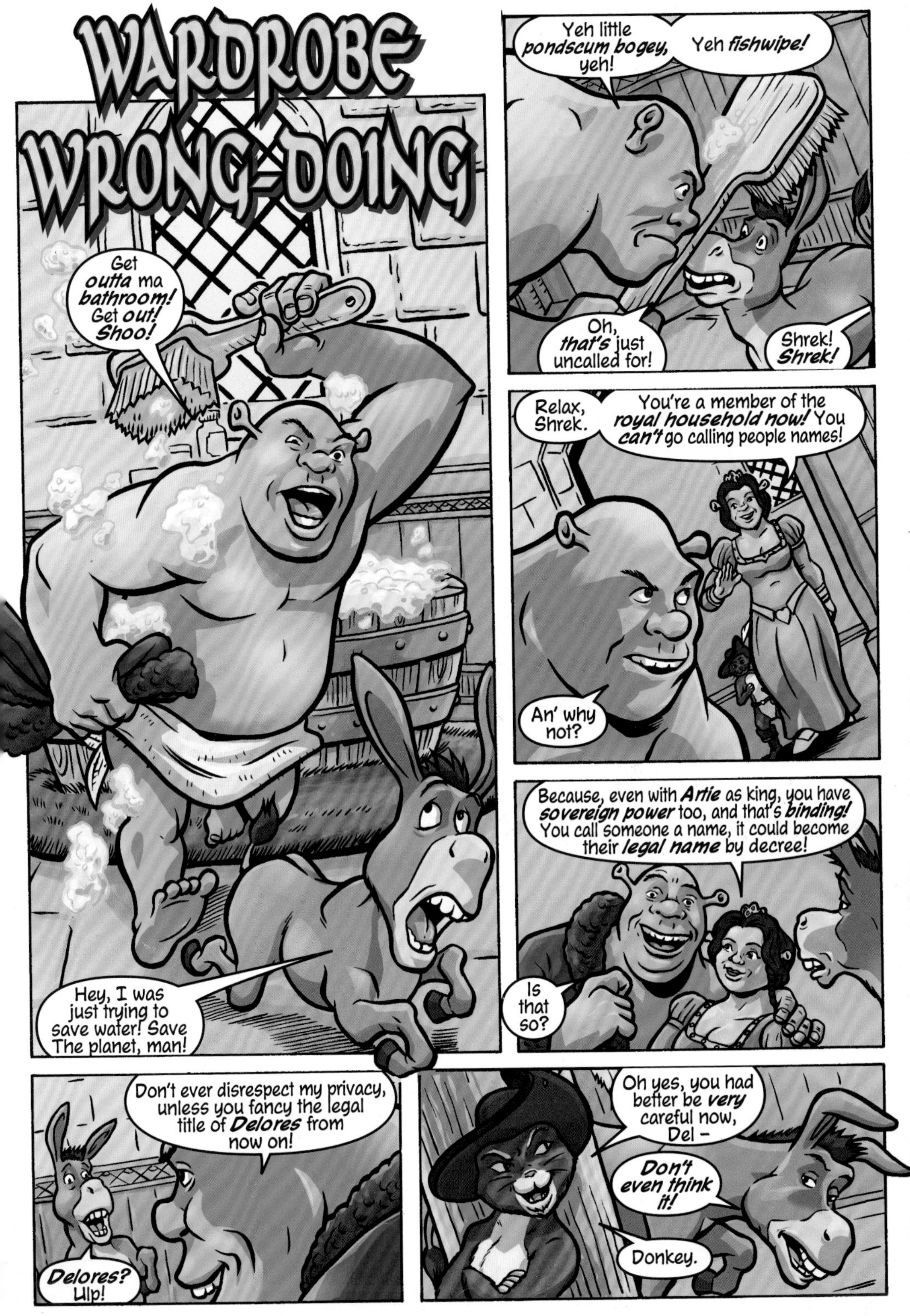

Get outta ma bathroom! Get out! Shoo!
Hey, I was just trying to save water! Save The planet, man!
Yeh little pondscum bogey, yeh!
Yeh fishwipe!
Oh, that's just uncalled for!
Shrek! Shrek!
Relax, Shrek.
You're a member of the royal household now! You can't go calling people names!
An' why not?
Because, even with Artie as king, you have sovereign power too, and that's binding! You call someone a name, it could become their legal name by decree!
Is that so?
Don't ever disrespect my privacy, unless you fancy the legal title of Delores from now on!
Delores? Ulp!
Oh yes, you had better be very careful now, Del –
Don't even think it!
Donkey.

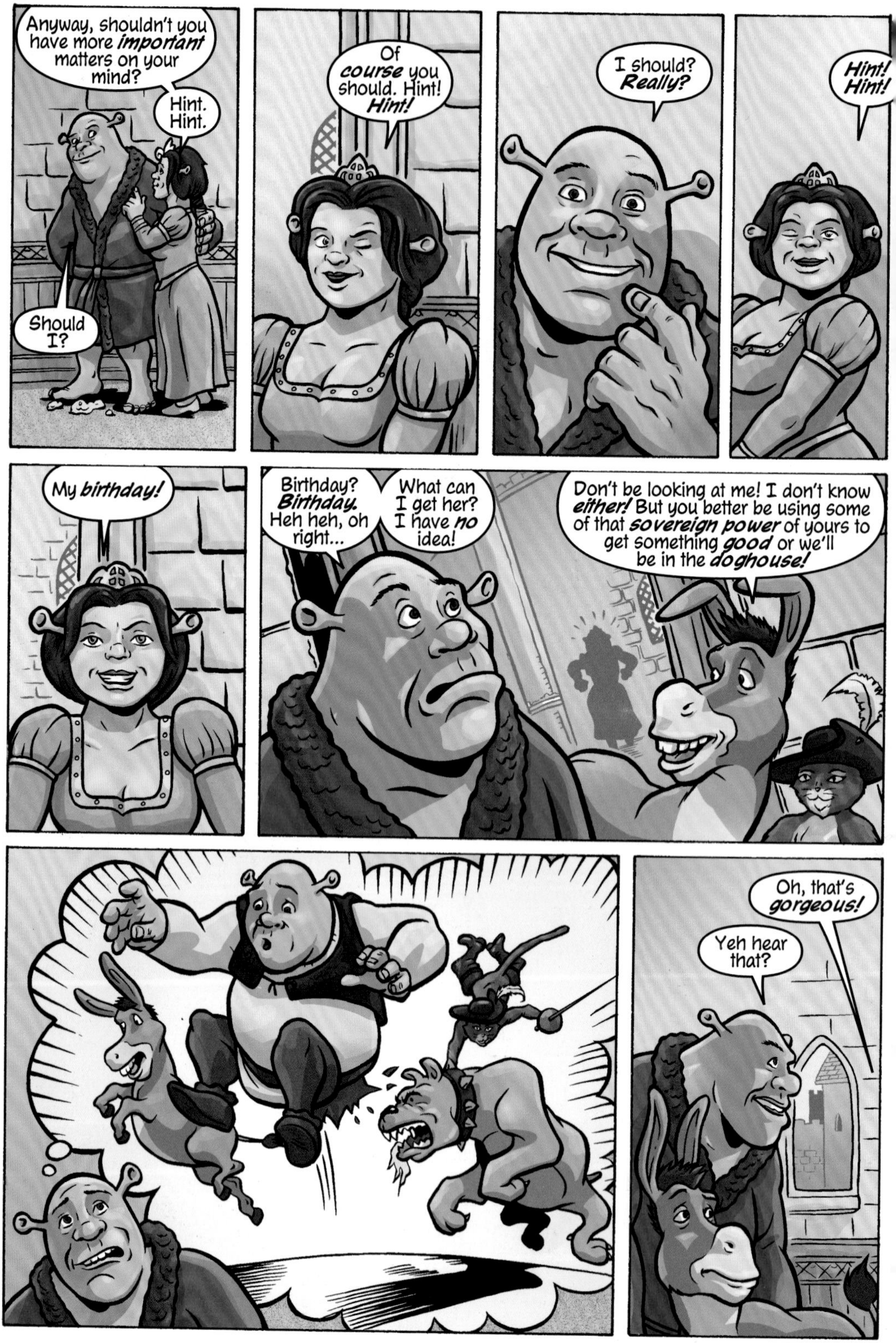

Anyway, shouldn't you have more *important* matters on your mind?
Hint. Hint.
Should I?
Of *course* you should. Hint! *Hint!*
I should? *Really?*
Hint! Hint!
My *birthday!*
Birthday? *Birthday.* Heh heh, oh right...
What can I get her? I have *no* idea!
Don't be looking at me! I don't know *either!* But you better be using some of that *sovereign power* of yours to get something *good* or we'll be in the *doghouse!*
Oh, that's *gorgeous!*
Yeh hear that?

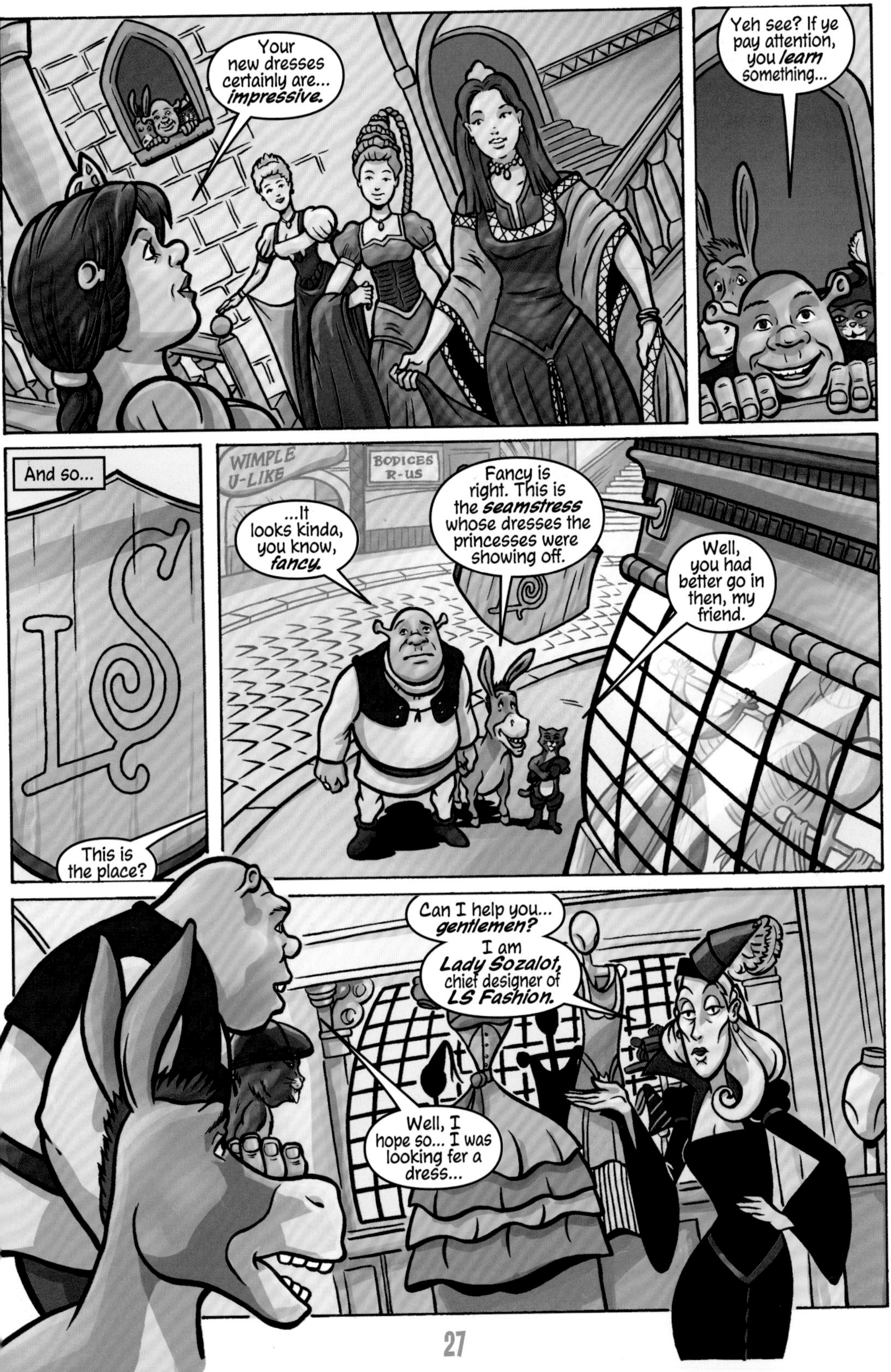

Your new dresses certainly are... *impressive.*
Yeh see? If ye pay attention, you *learn* something...
And so...
This is the place?
WIMPLE U-LIKE
BODICES R-US
...It looks kinda, you know, *fancy.*
Fancy is right. This is the *seamstress* whose dresses the princesses were showing off.
Well, you had better go in then, my friend.
Can I help you... *gentlemen?*
I am *Lady Sozalot,* chief designer of *LS Fashion.*
Well, I hope so... I was looking fer a dress...

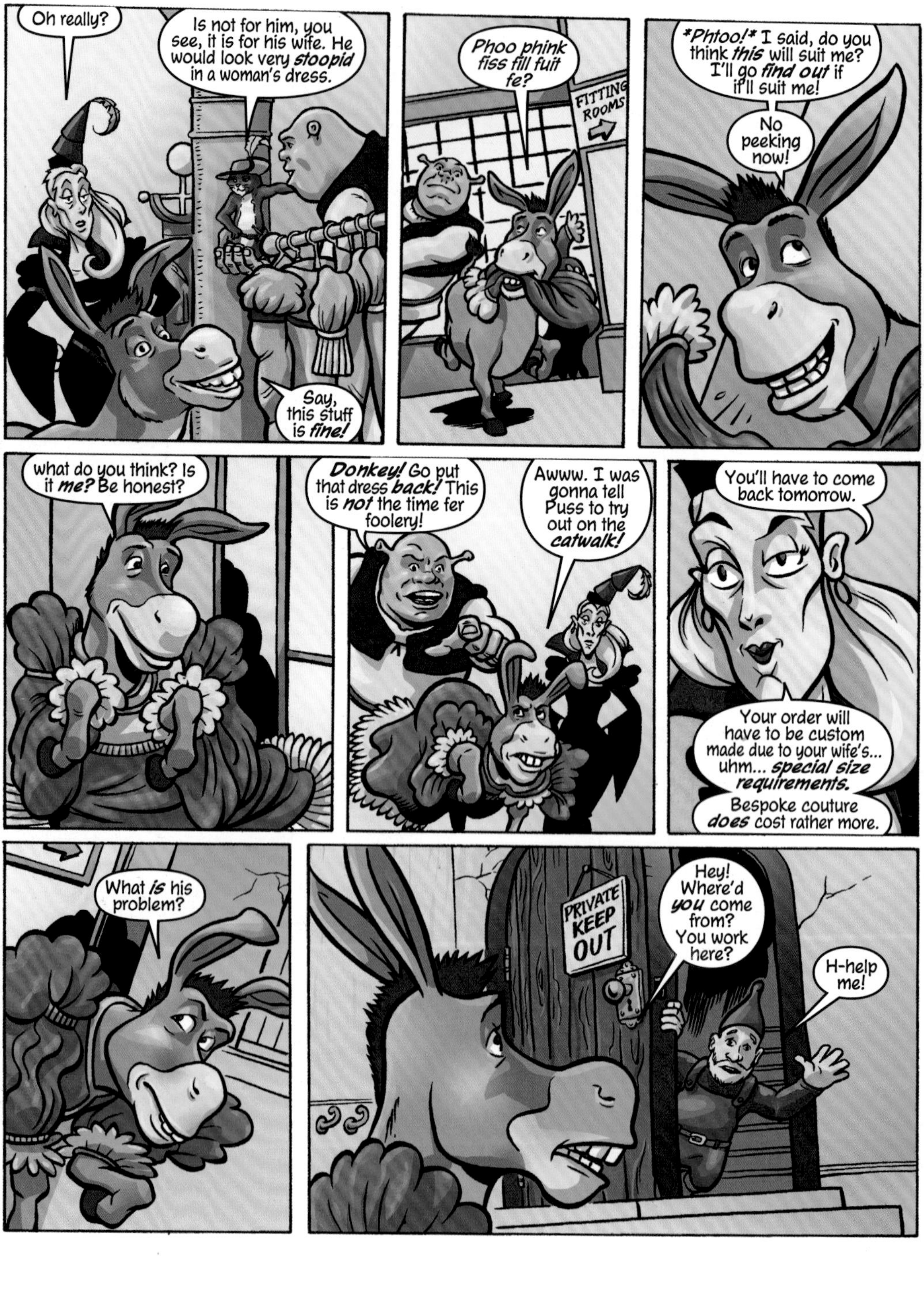

Oh really?
Is not for him, you see, it is for his wife. He would look very stoopid in a woman's dress.
Say, this stuff is fine!
Phoo phink fiss fill fuit fe?
FITTING ROOMS
Phtoo! I said, do you think this will suit me? I'll go find out if it'll suit me!
No peeking now!
what do you think? Is it me? Be honest?
Donkey! Go put that dress back! This is not the time fer foolery!
Awww. I was gonna tell Puss to try out on the catwalk!
You'll have to come back tomorrow.
Your order will have to be custom made due to your wife's... uhm... special size requirements.
Bespoke couture does cost rather more.
What is his problem?
PRIVATE KEEP OUT
Hey! Where'd you come from? You work here?
H-help me!

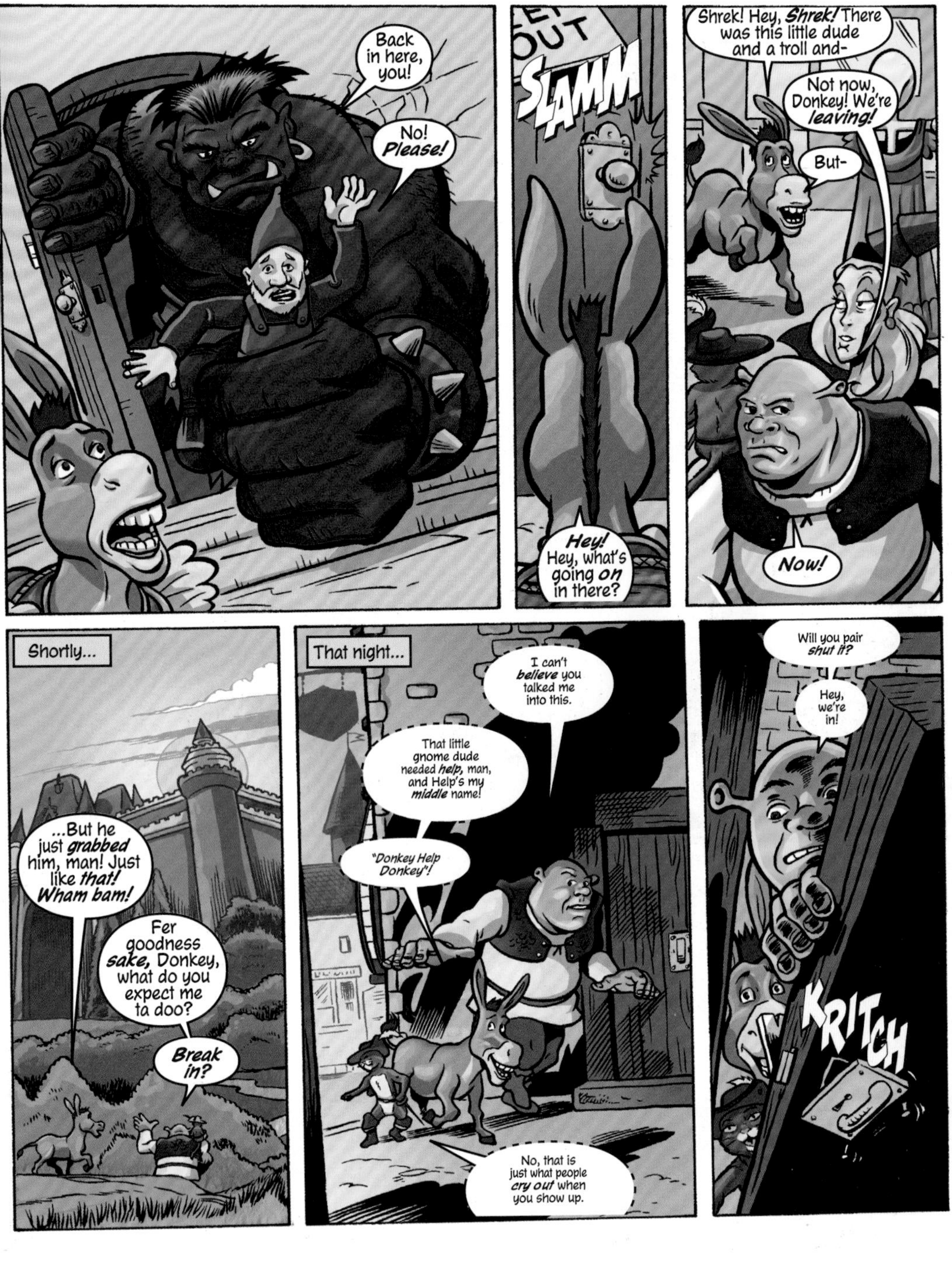

Back in here, you!
No! Please!
SLAMM
Hey! Hey, what's going on in there?
Shrek! Hey, Shrek! There was this little dude and a troll and-
Not now, Donkey! We're leaving!
But-
Now!
Shortly...
...But he just grabbed him, man! Just like that! Wham bam!
Fer goodness sake, Donkey, what do you expect me ta doo?
Break in?
That night...
I can't believe you talked me into this.
That little gnome dude needed help, man, and Help's my middle name!
"Donkey Help Donkey"!
No, that is just what people cry out when you show up.
Will you pair shut it?
Hey, we're in!
KRITCH

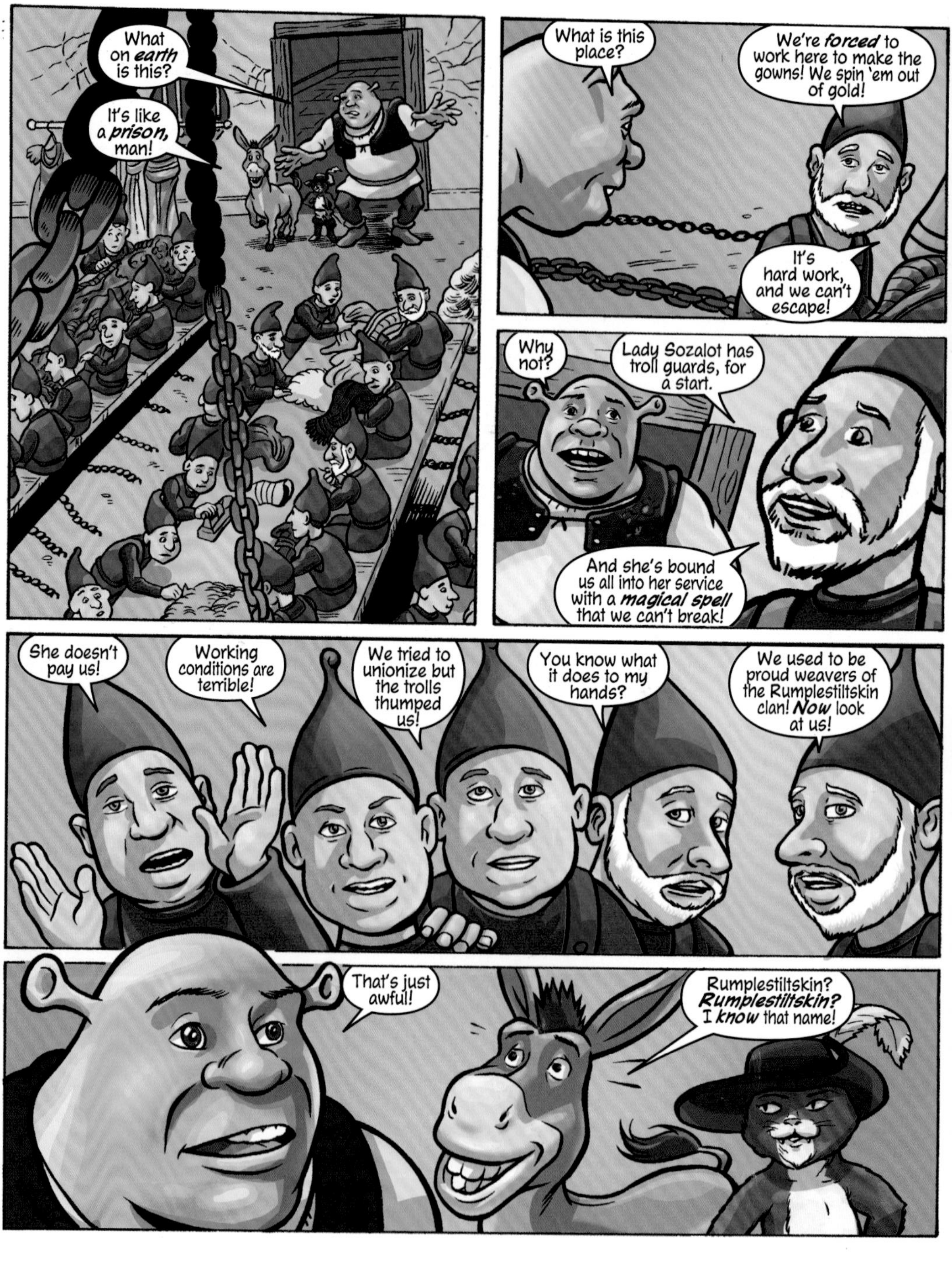
What on earth is this?
It's like a prison, man!
What is this place?
We're forced to work here to make the gowns! We spin 'em out of gold!
It's hard work, and we can't escape!
Why not?
Lady Sozalot has troll guards, for a start.
And she's bound us all into her service with a magical spell that we can't break!
She doesn't pay us!
Working conditions are terrible!
We tried to unionize but the trolls thumped us!
You know what it does to my hands?
We used to be proud weavers of the Rumplestiltskin clan! Now look at us!
That's just awful!
Rumplestiltskin? Rumplestiltskin? I know that name!

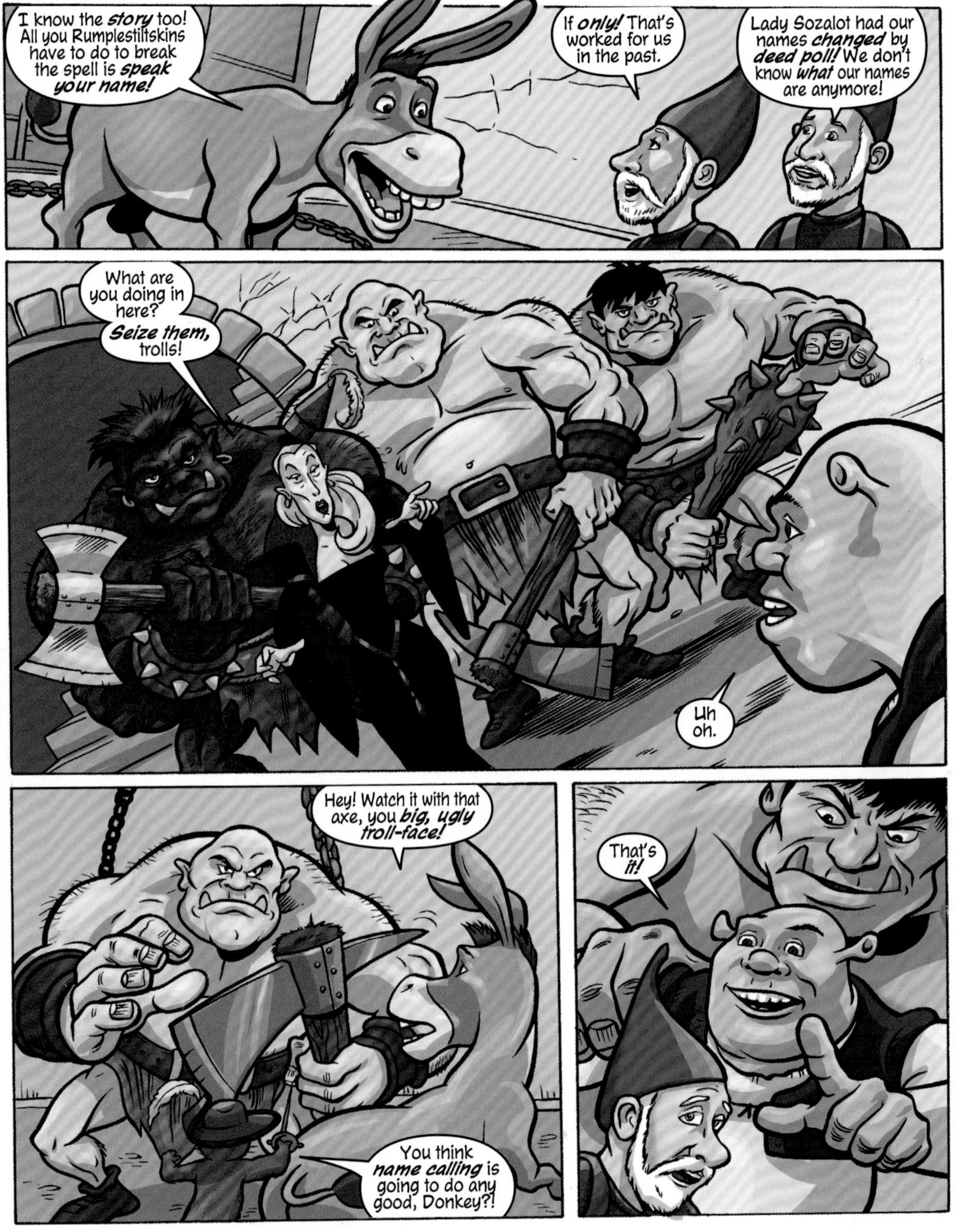
I know the *story* too! All you Rumplestiltskins have to do to break the spell is *speak your name!*
If *only!* That's worked for us in the past.
Lady Sozalot had our names *changed* by *deed poll!* We don't know *what* our names are anymore!
What are you doing in here? *Seize them,* trolls!
Uh oh.
Hey! Watch it with that axe, you *big, ugly troll-face!*
You think *name calling* is going to do any good, Donkey?!
That's *it!*

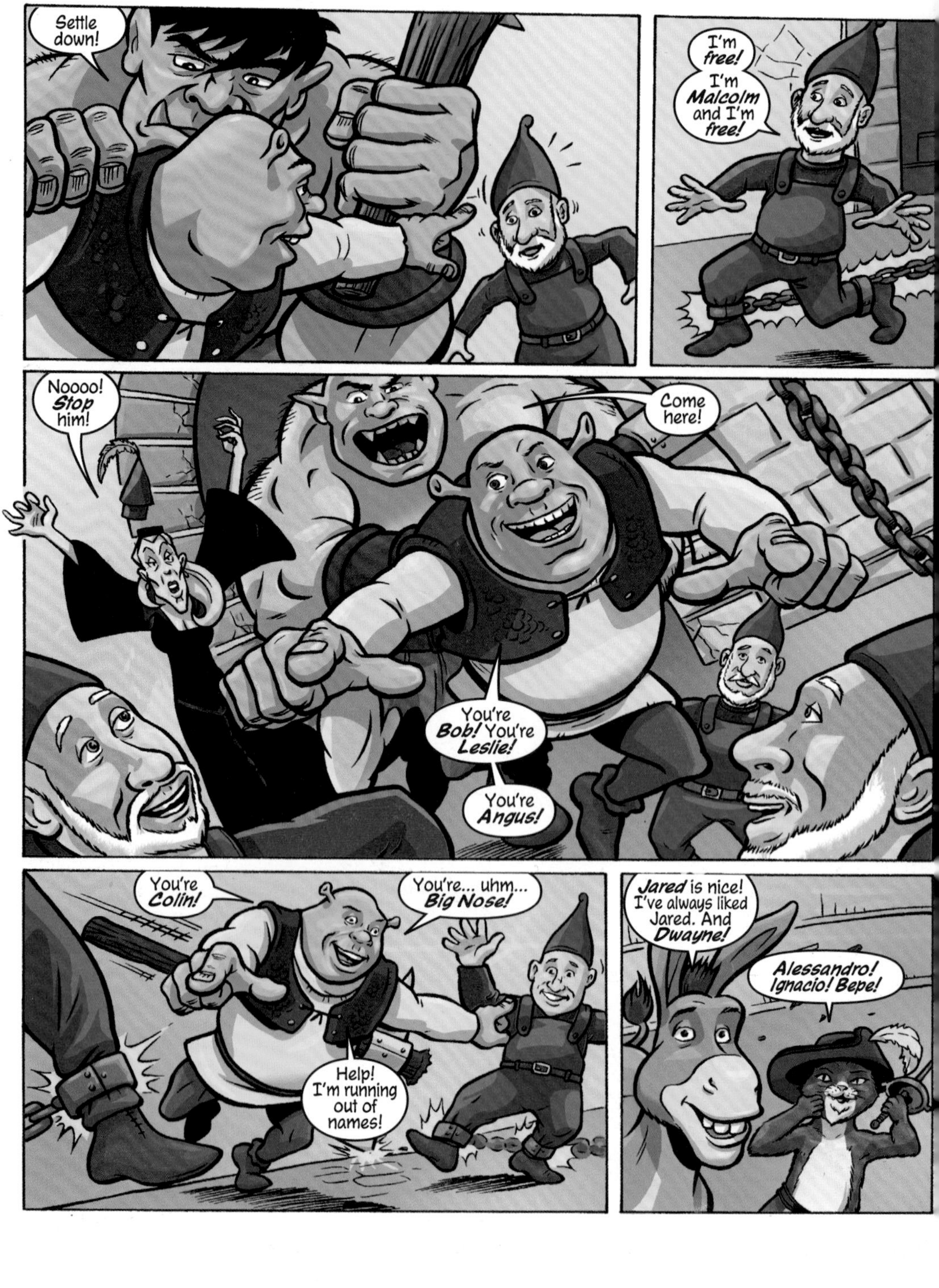
Settle down!
I'm free! I'm Malcolm and I'm free!
Noooo! Stop him!
Come here!
You're Bob! You're Leslie!
You're Angus!
You're Colin!
You're... uhm... Big Nose!
Help! I'm running out of names!
Jared is nice! I've always liked Jared. And Dwayne!
Alessandro! Ignacio! Bepe!

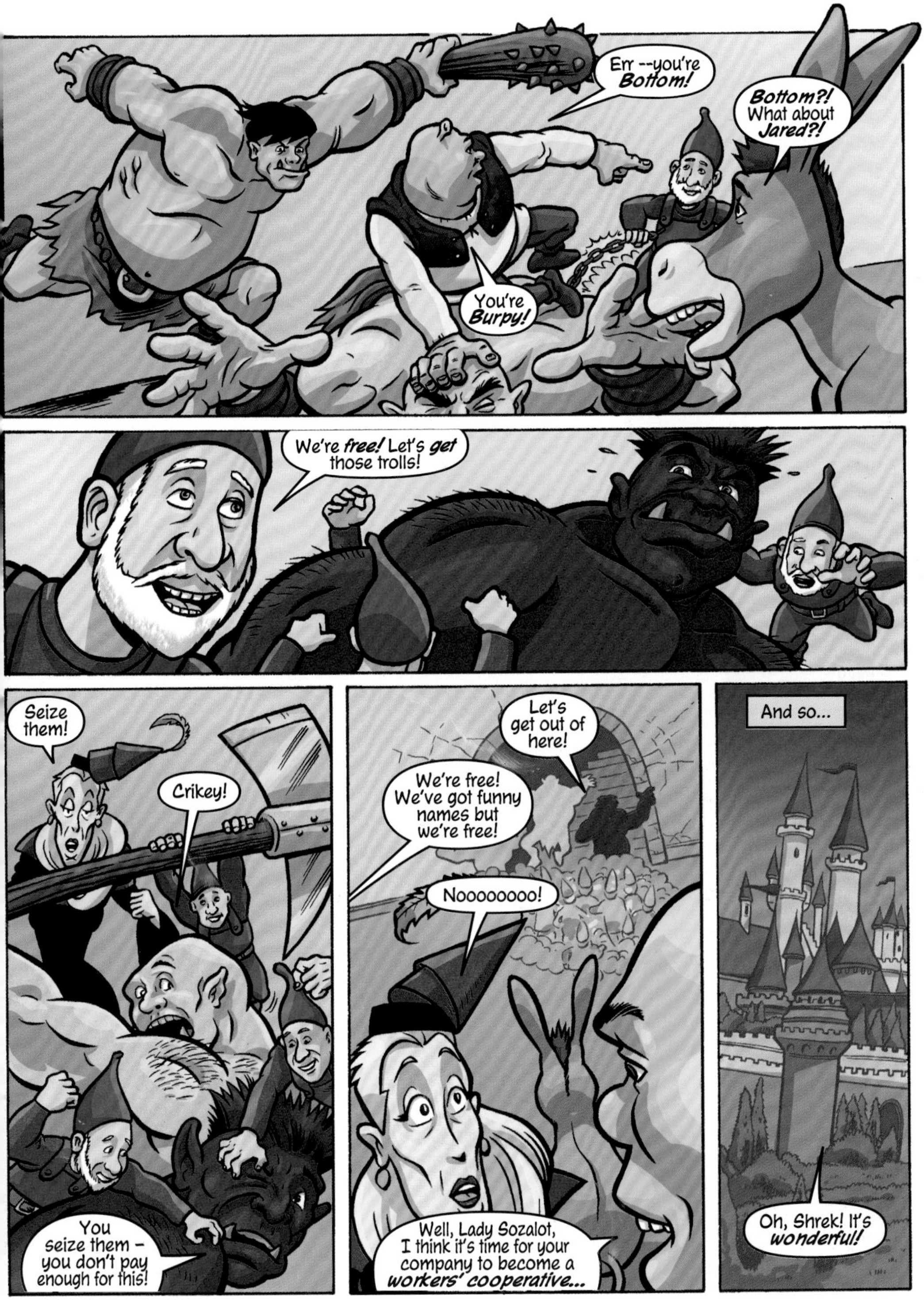
Err --you're Bottom!
Bottom?! What about Jared?!
You're Burpy!
We're free! Let's get those trolls!
Seize them!
Crikey!
You seize them - you don't pay enough for this!
Let's get out of here!
We're free! We've got funny names but we're free!
Noooooooo!
Well, Lady Sozalot, I think it's time for your company to become a workers' cooperative...
And so...
Oh, Shrek! It's wonderful!

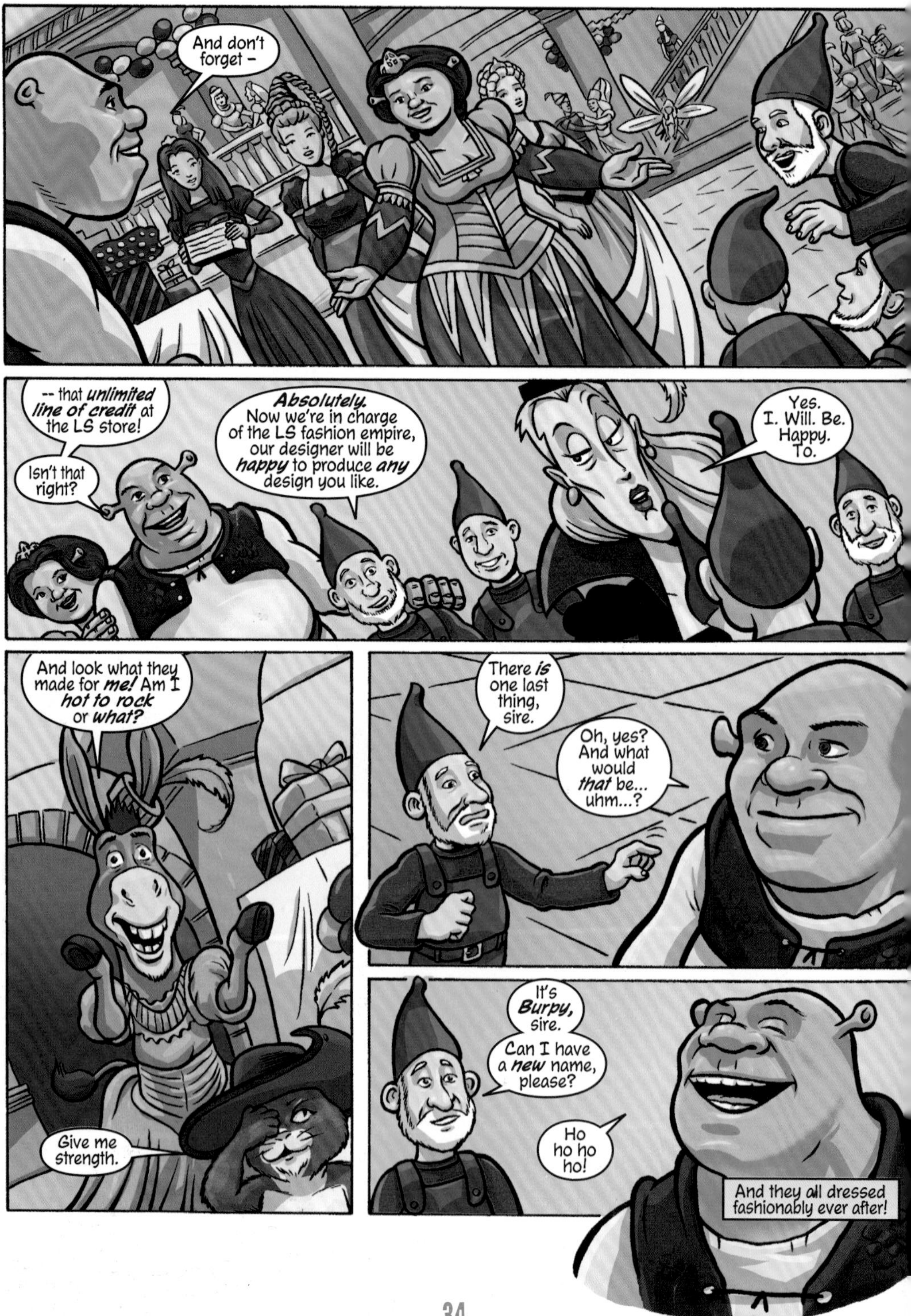
And don't forget –
-- that *unlimited line of credit* at the LS store!
Isn't that right?
Absolutely. Now we're in charge of the LS fashion empire, our designer will be *happy* to produce *any* design you like.
Yes. I. Will. Be. Happy. To.
And look what they made for *me!* Am I *hot to rock* or *what?*
Give me strength.
There *is* one last thing, sire.
Oh, yes? And what would *that* be... uhm...?
It's *Burpy,* sire.
Can I have a *new* name, please?
Ho ho ho ho!
And they all dressed fashionably ever after!

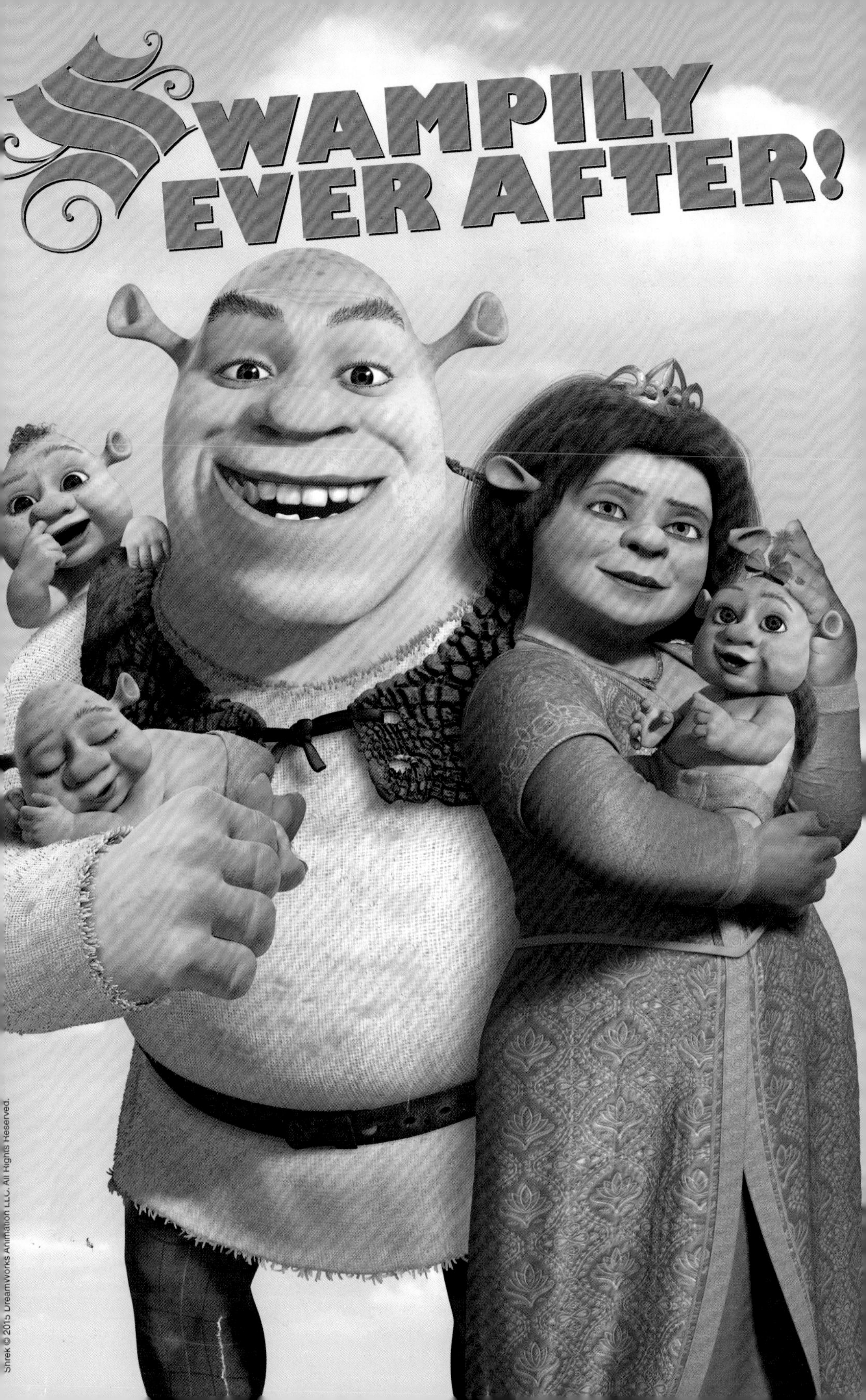
SWAMPILY
EVER AFTER!

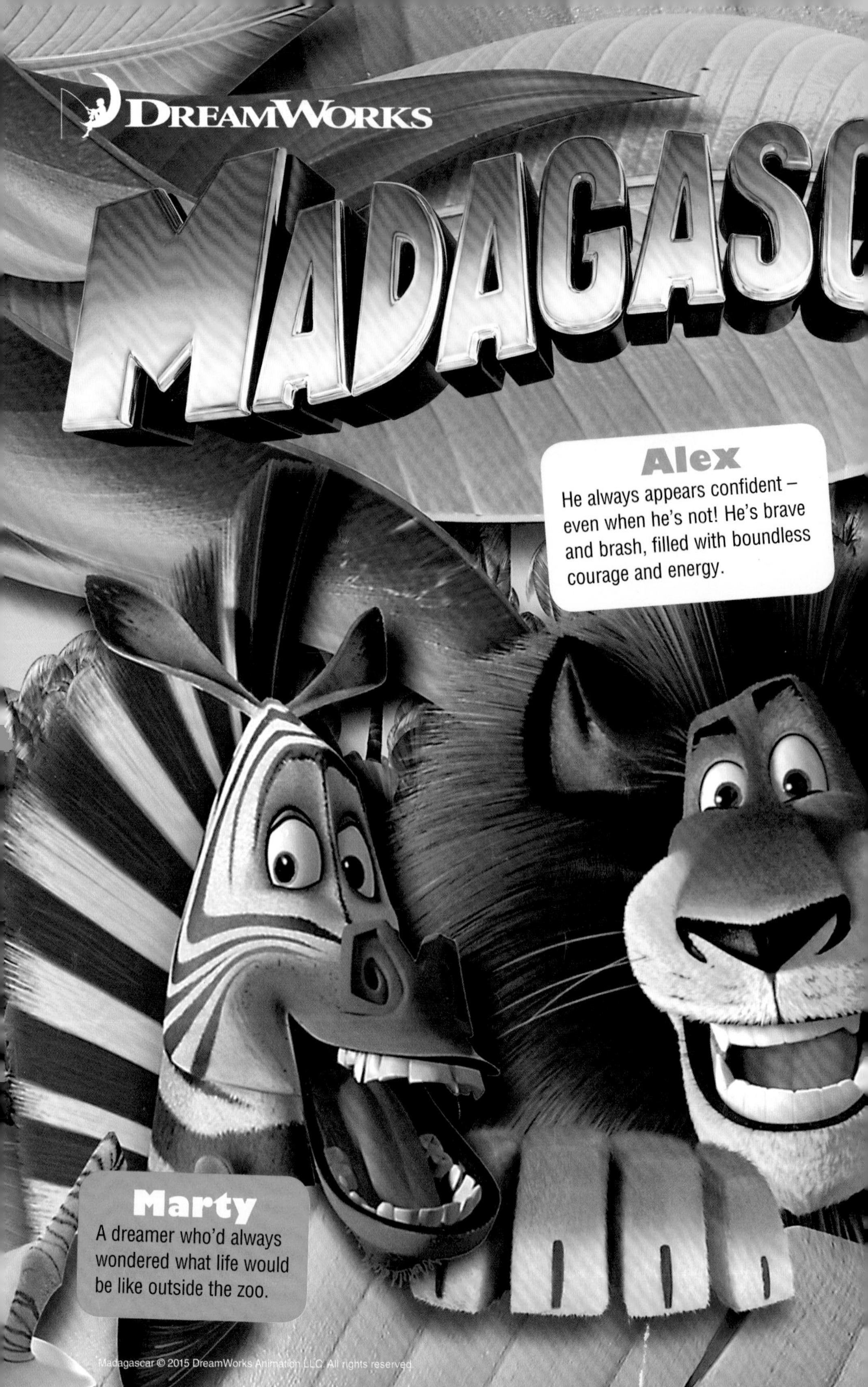
DreamWorks
Alex
He always appears confident – even when he's not! He's brave and brash, filled with boundless courage and energy.
Marty
A dreamer who'd always wondered what life would be like outside the zoo.

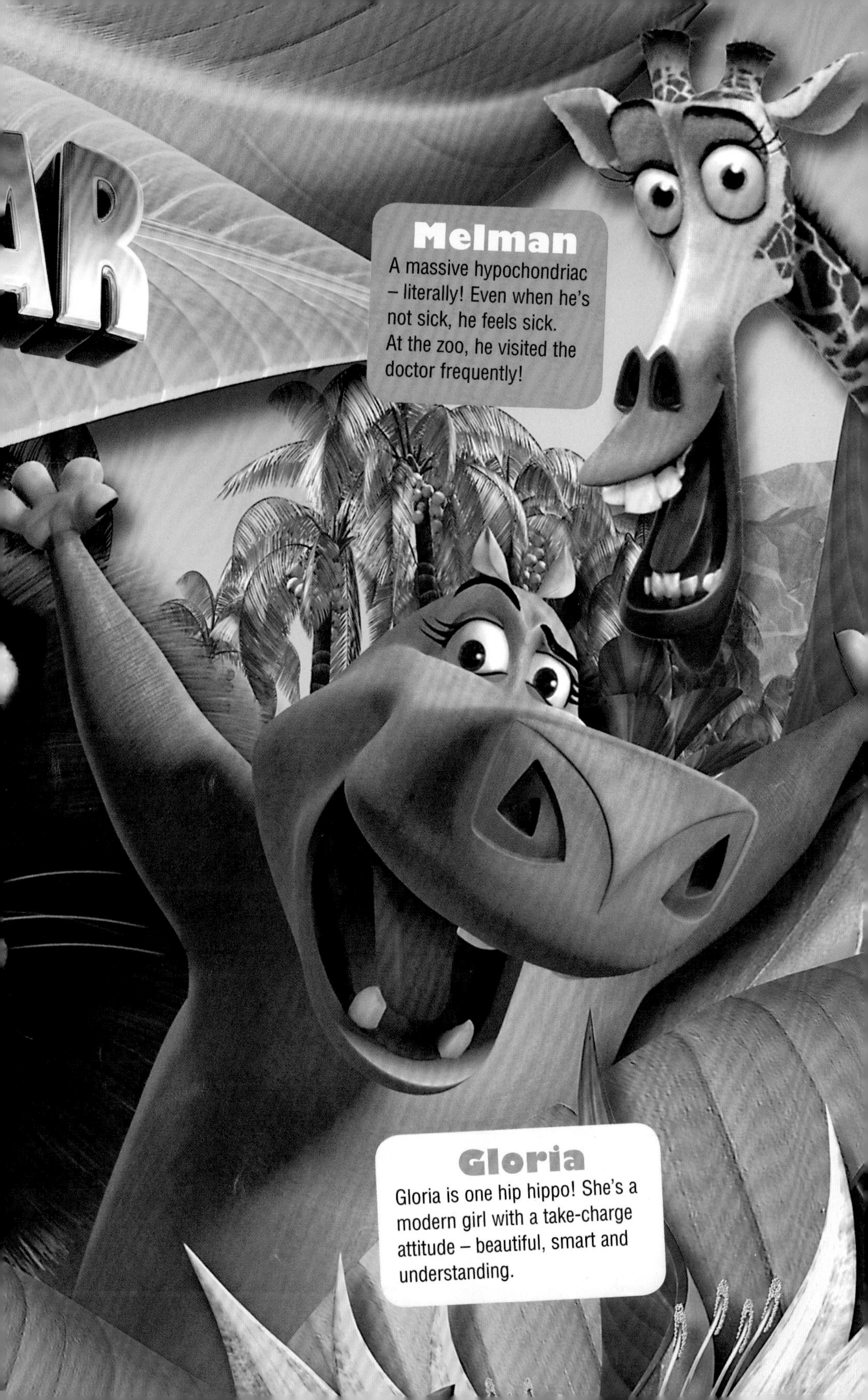

Melman

A massive hypochondriac – literally! Even when he's not sick, he feels sick. At the zoo, he visited the doctor frequently!

Gloria

Gloria is one hip hippo! She's a modern girl with a take-charge attitude – beautiful, smart and understanding.

HIDE & SEEK

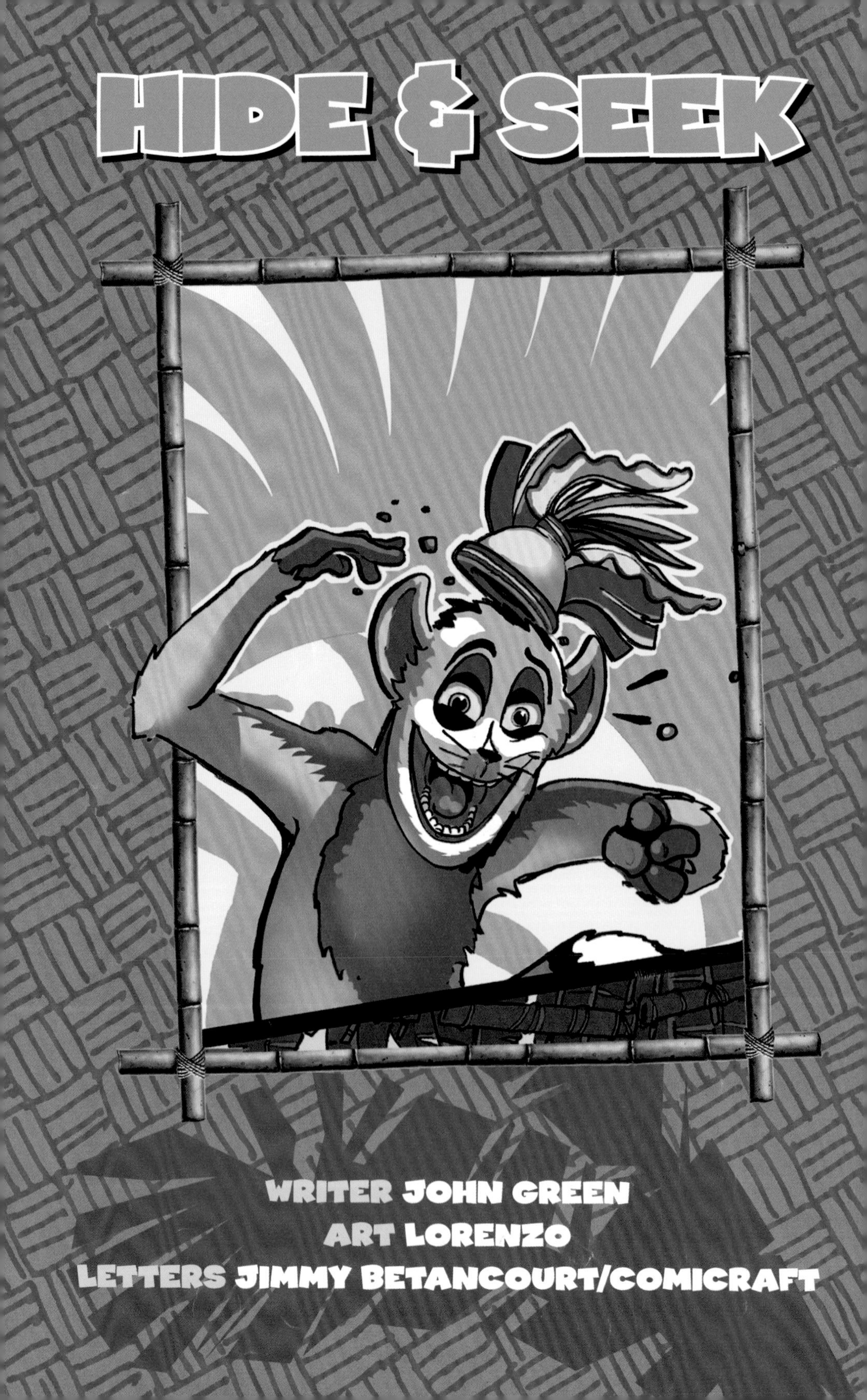

WRITER JOHN GREEN
ART LORENZO
LETTERS JIMMY BETANCOURT/COMICRAFT

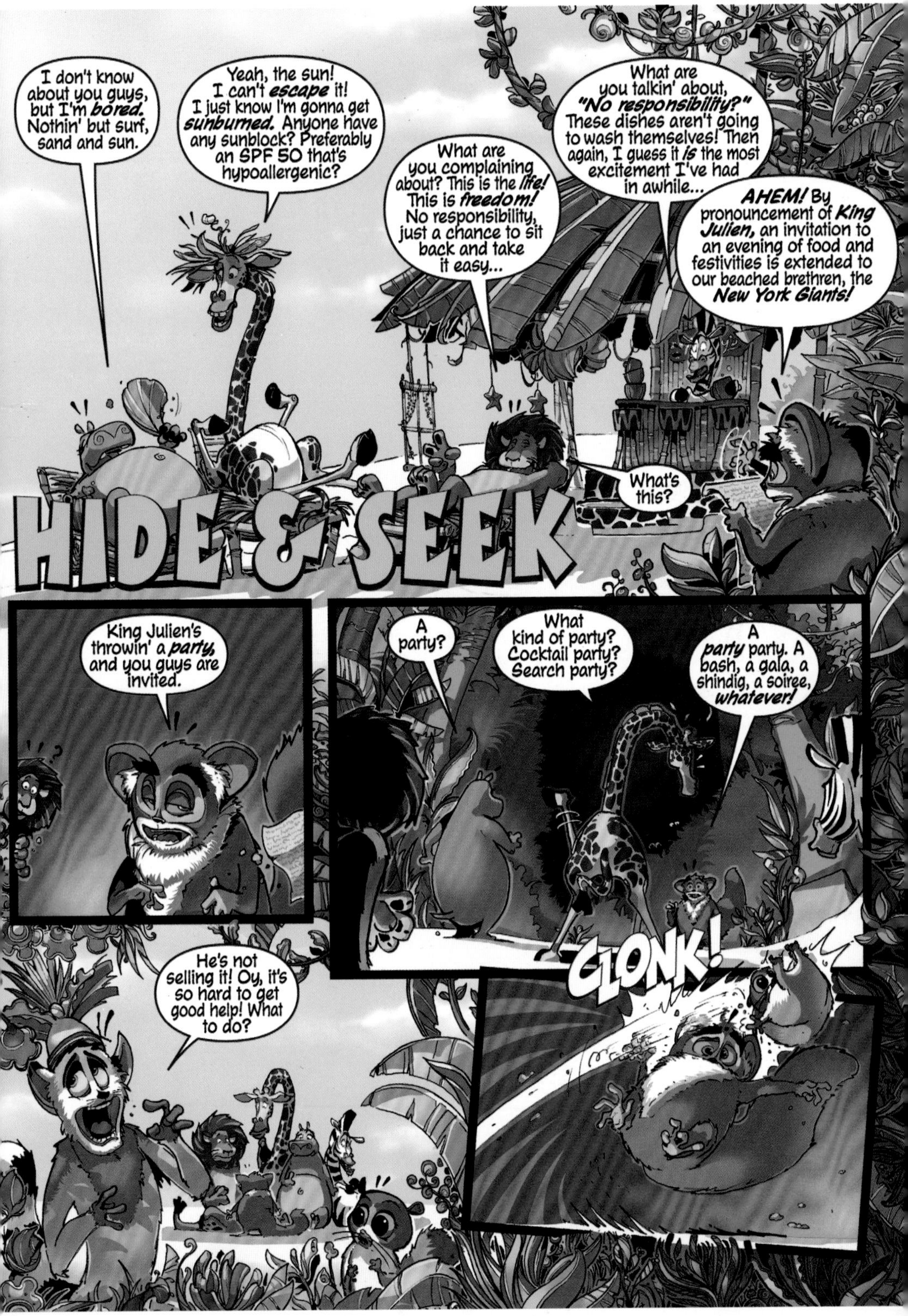
I don't know about you guys, but I'm bored. Nothin' but surf, sand and sun.
Yeah, the sun! I can't escape it! I just know I'm gonna get sunburned. Anyone have any sunblock? Preferably an SPF 50 that's hypoallergenic?
What are you complaining about? This is the life! This is freedom! No responsibility, just a chance to sit back and take it easy...
What are you talkin' about, "No responsibility?" These dishes aren't going to wash themselves! Then again, I guess it is the most excitement I've had in awhile...
AHEM! By pronouncement of King Julien, an invitation to an evening of food and festivities is extended to our beached brethren, the New York Giants!
What's this?
HIDE & SEEK
King Julien's throwin' a party, and you guys are invited.
A party?
What kind of party? Cocktail party? Search party?
A party party. A bash, a gala, a shindig, a soiree, whatever!
CLONK!
He's not selling it! Oy, it's so hard to get good help! What to do?

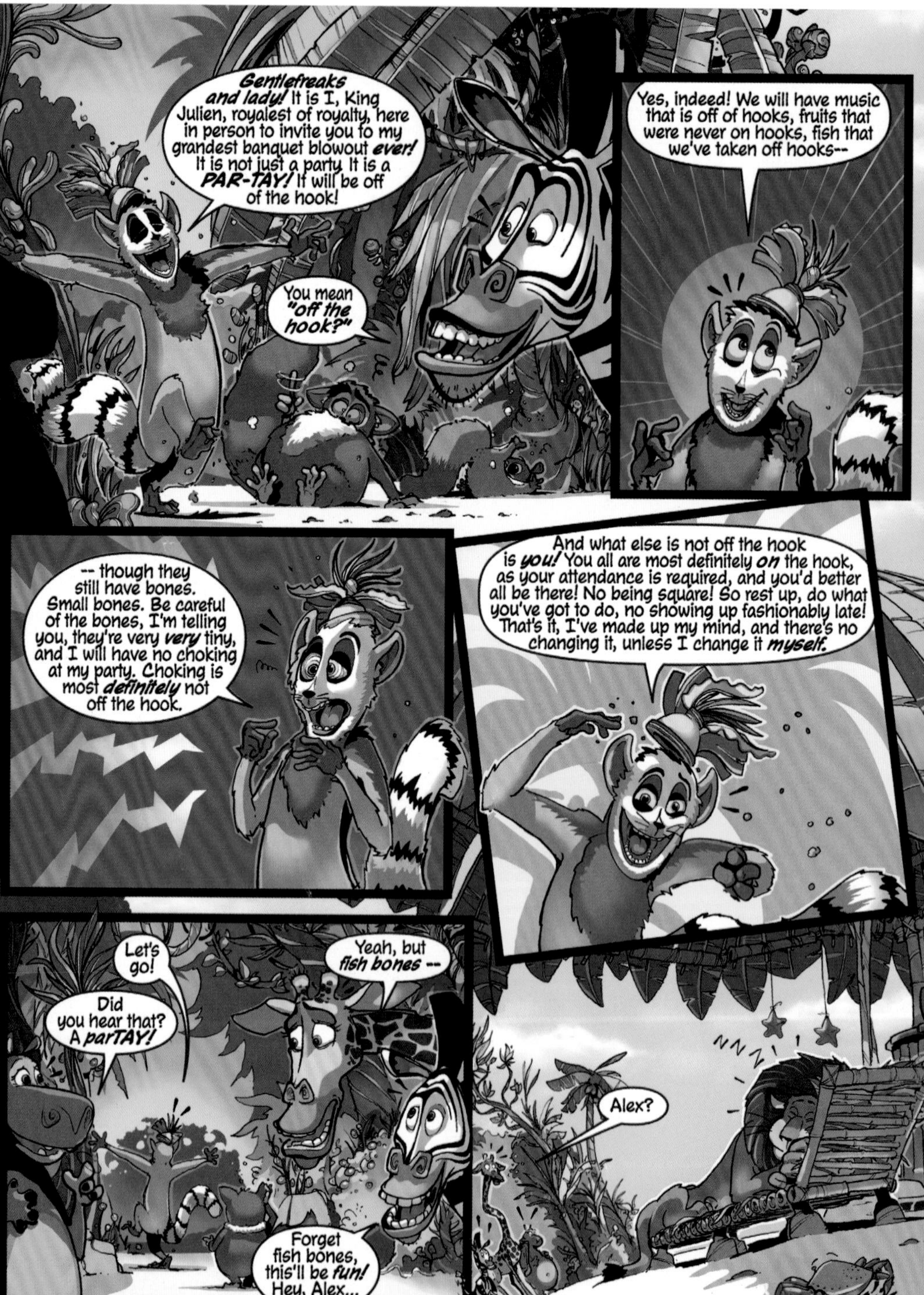
Gentlefreaks and lady! It is I, King Julien, royalest of royalty, here in person to invite you to my grandest banquet blowout ever! It is not just a party. It is a PAR-TAY! It will be off of the hook!
You mean "off the hook?"
Yes, indeed! We will have music that is off of hooks, fruits that were never on hooks, fish that we've taken off hooks--
-- though they still have bones. Small bones. Be careful of the bones, I'm telling you, they're very very tiny, and I will have no choking at my party. Choking is most definitely not off the hook.
And what else is not off the hook is you! You all are most definitely on the hook, as your attendance is required, and you'd better all be there! No being square! So rest up, do what you've got to do, no showing up fashionably late! That's it, I've made up my mind, and there's no changing it, unless I change it myself.
Let's go!
Did you hear that? A parTAY!
Yeah, but fish bones --
Forget fish bones, this'll be fun! Hey, Alex...
NNN
Alex?

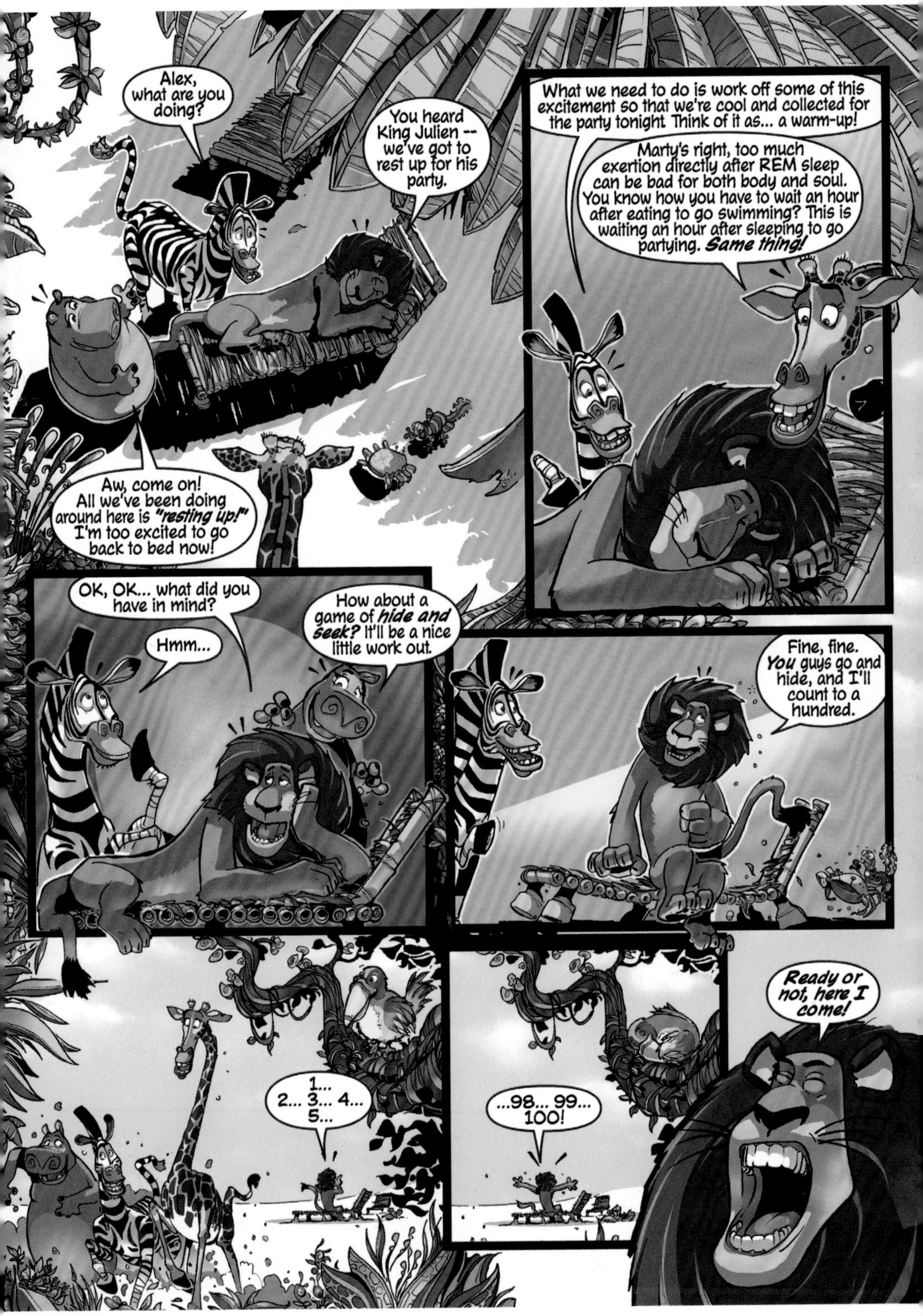
Alex, what are you doing?
You heard King Julien -- we've got to rest up for his party.
Aw, come on! All we've been doing around here is "resting up!" I'm too excited to go back to bed now!
What we need to do is work off some of this excitement so that we're cool and collected for the party tonight. Think of it as... a warm-up!
Marty's right, too much exertion directly after REM sleep can be bad for both body and soul. You know how you have to wait an hour after eating to go swimming? This is waiting an hour after sleeping to go partying. Same thing!
OK, OK... what did you have in mind?
Hmm...
How about a game of hide and seek? It'll be a nice little work out.
Fine, fine. You guys go and hide, and I'll count to a hundred.
1... 2... 3... 4... 5...
...98... 99... 100!
Ready or not, here I come!

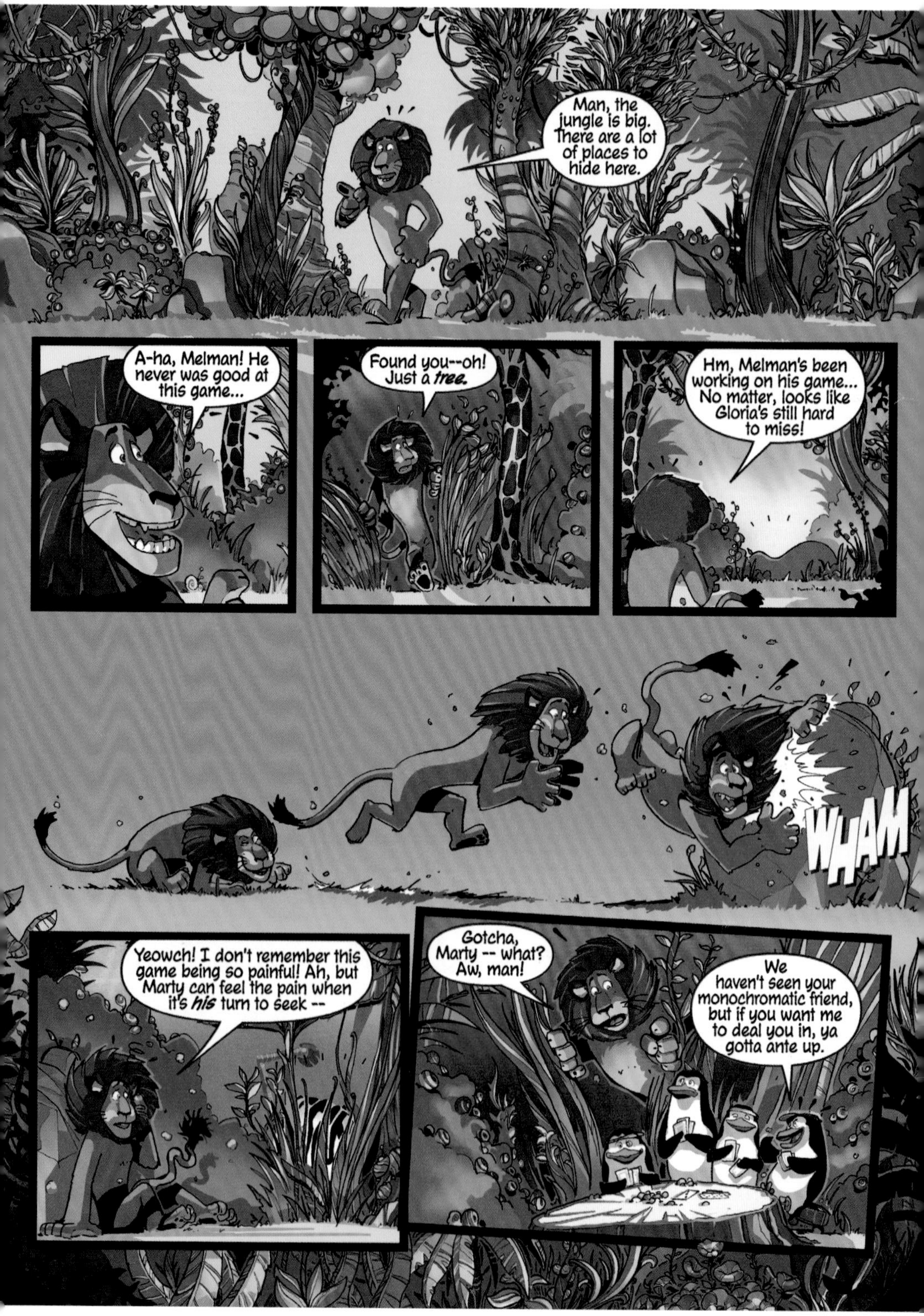
Man, the jungle is big. There are a lot of places to hide here.
A-ha, Melman! He never was good at this game...
Found you--oh! Just a *tree*.
Hm, Melman's been working on his game... No matter, looks like Gloria's still hard to miss!
WHAM
Yeowch! I don't remember this game being so painful! Ah, but Marty can feel the pain when it's *his* turn to seek --
Gotcha, Marty -- what? Aw, man!
We haven't seen your monochromatic friend, but if you want me to deal you in, ya gotta ante up.

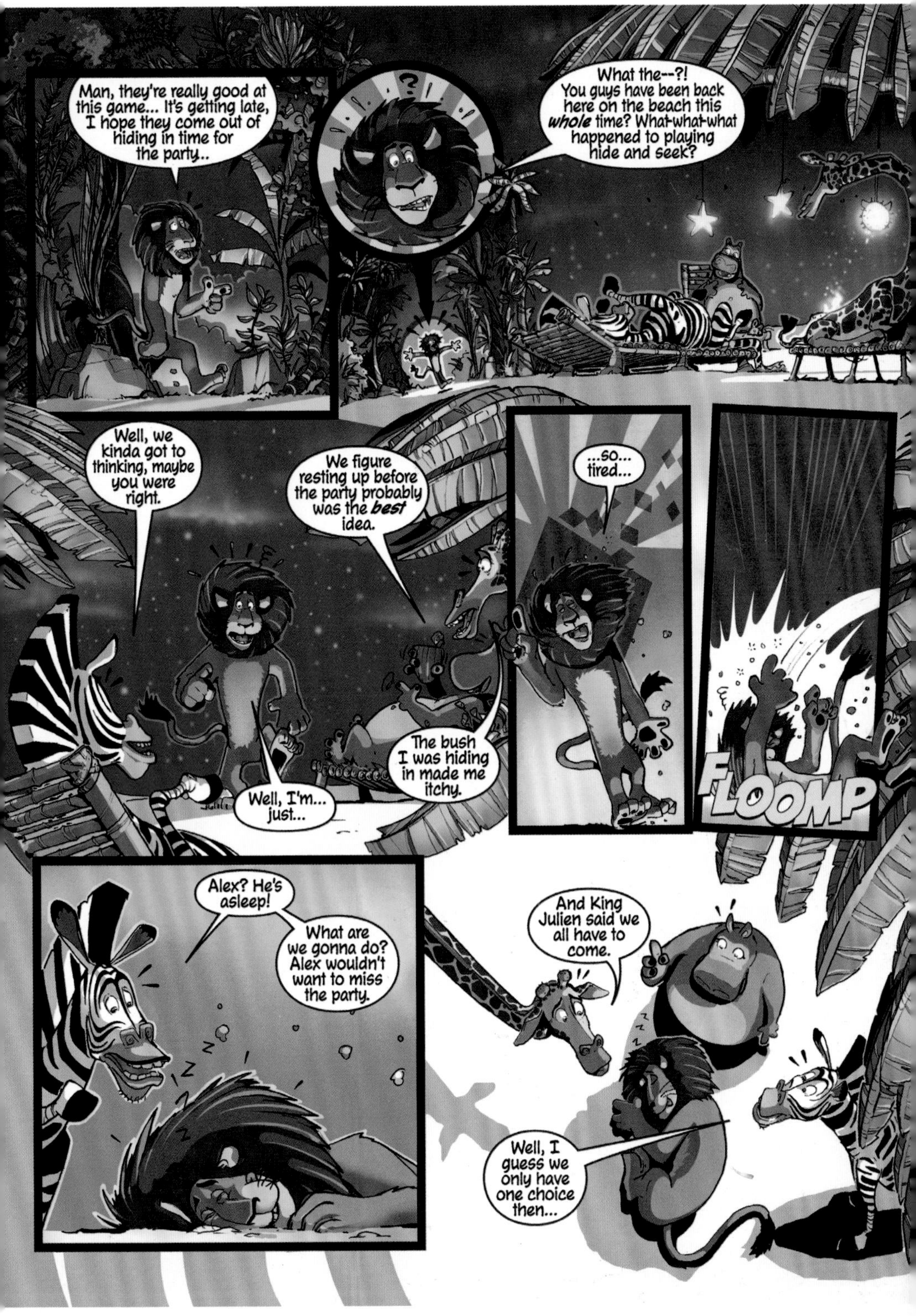

Man, they're really good at this game... It's getting late, I hope they come out of hiding in time for the party..
?
What the--?! You guys have been back here on the beach this *whole* time? What-what-what happened to playing hide and seek?
Well, we kinda got to thinking, maybe you were right.
We figure resting up before the party probably was the *best* idea.
The bush I was hiding in made me itchy.
Well, I'm... just...
...so... tired...
FLOOMP
Alex? He's asleep!
What are we gonna do? Alex wouldn't want to miss the party.
And King Julien said we all have to come.
Well, I guess we only have one choice then...

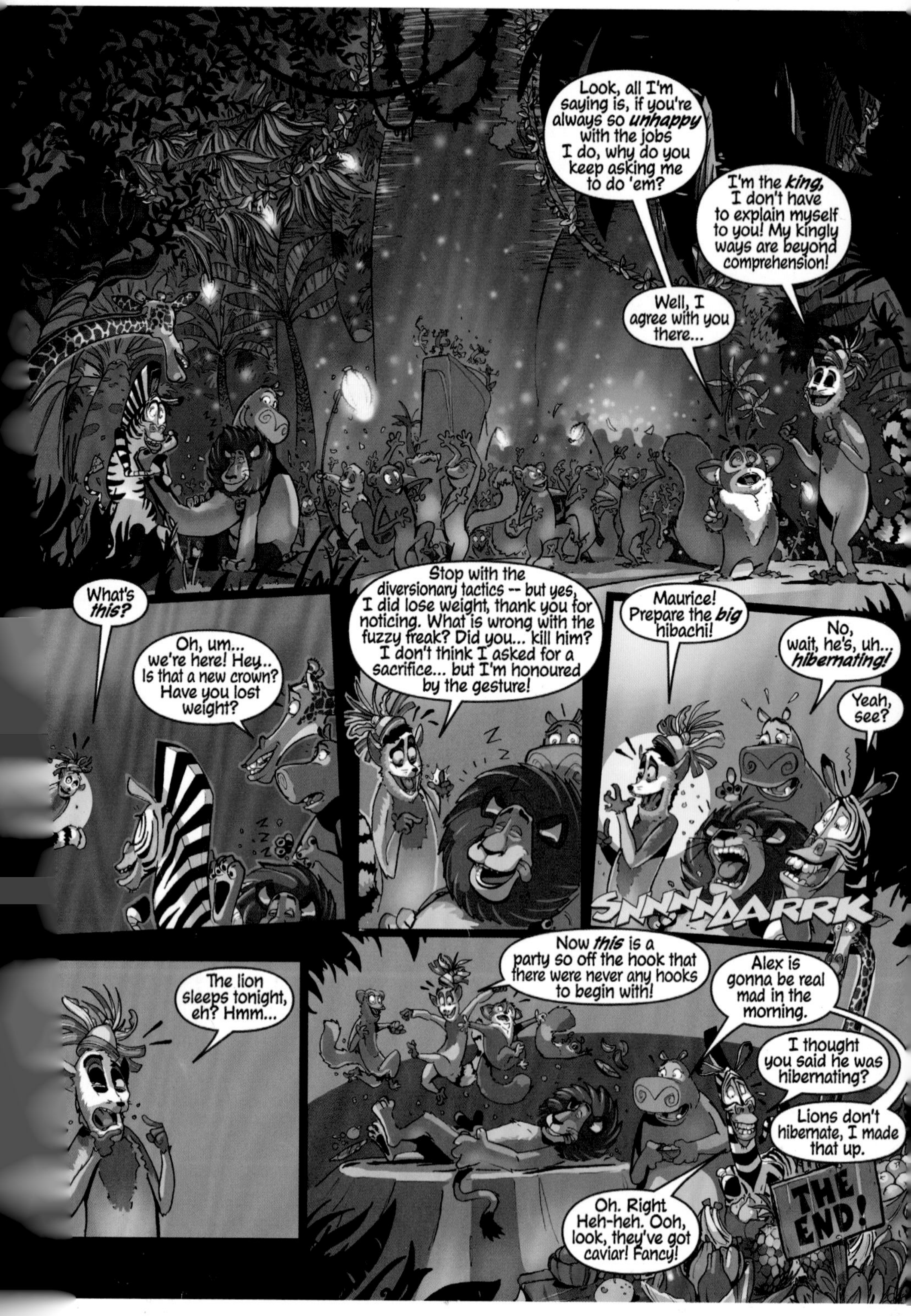

Look, all I'm saying is, if you're always so *unhappy* with the jobs I do, why do you keep asking me to do 'em?
I'm the *king,* I don't have to explain myself to you! My kingly ways are beyond comprehension!
Well, I agree with you there...
What's *this?*
Oh, um... we're here! Hey.. Is that a new crown? Have you lost weight?
Stop with the diversionary tactics -- but yes, I did lose weight, thank you for noticing. What is wrong with the fuzzy freak? Did you... kill him? I don't think I asked for a sacrifice... but I'm honoured by the gesture!
Maurice! Prepare the *big* hibachi!
No, wait, he's, uh... *hibernating!*
Yeah, see?
SNNNNDAARRK
The lion sleeps tonight, eh? Hmm...
Now *this* is a party so off the hook that there were never any hooks to begin with!
Alex is gonna be real mad in the morning.
I thought you said he was hibernating?
Lions don't hibernate, I made that up.
Oh. Right Heh-heh. Ooh, look, they've got caviar! Fancy!
THE END!

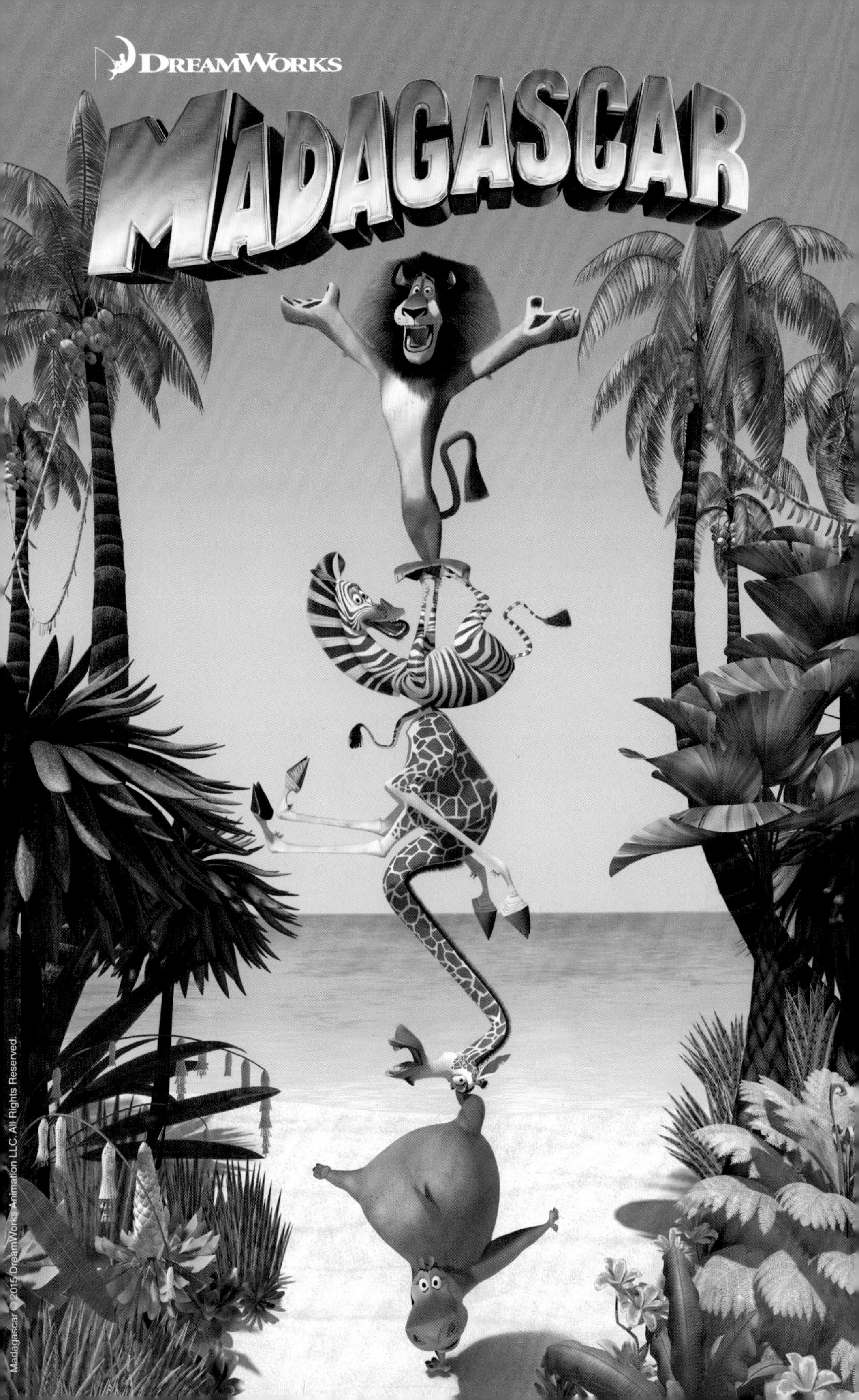
DreamWorks
MADAGASCAR

A PEACEFUL NIGHT'S SLEEP

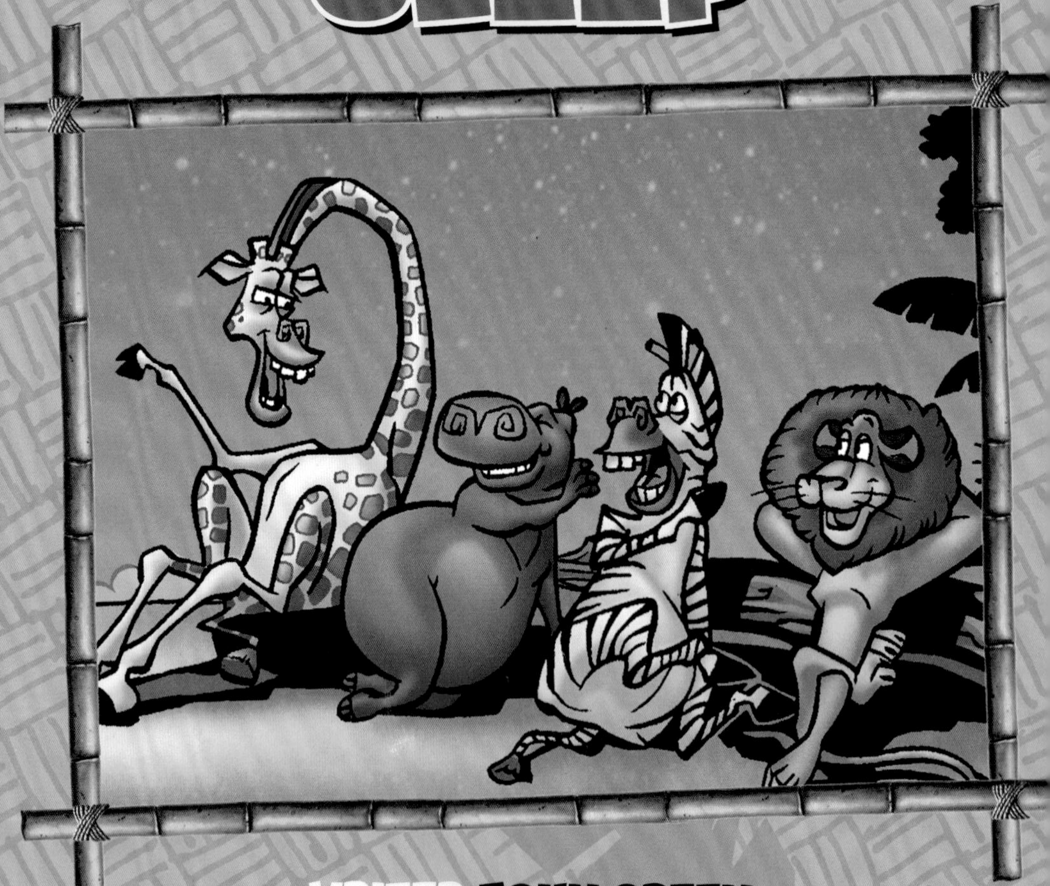

WRITER JOHN GREEN
PENCILS RICHARDO LEITE
INKS BAMBOS GEORGIOU
COLORS HI-FI COLOR DESIGN
LETTERS ALBERT DESCHESNE/COMICRAFT

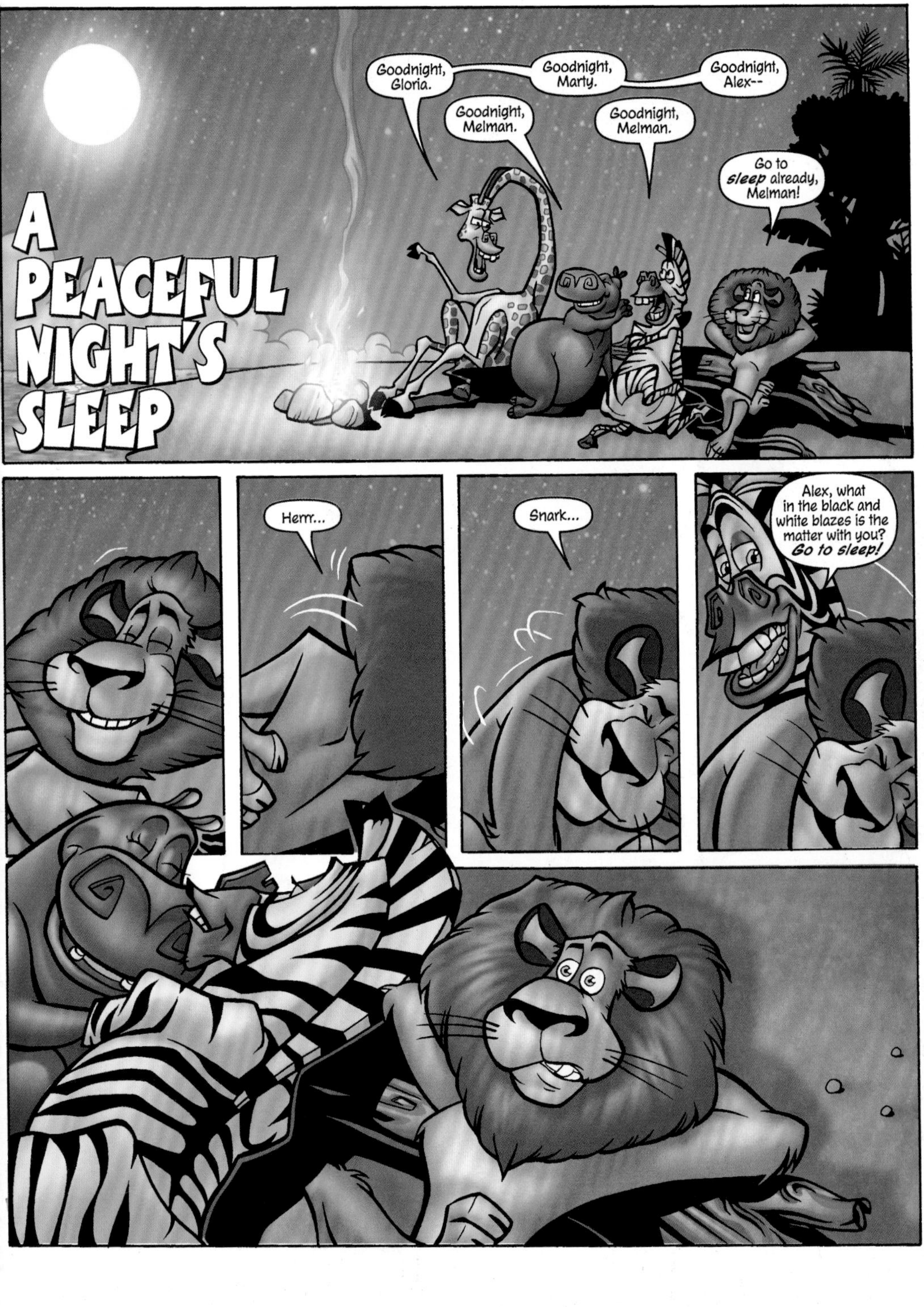
A PEACEFUL NIGHT'S SLEEP
Goodnight, Gloria.
Goodnight, Marty.
Goodnight, Alex--
Goodnight, Melman.
Goodnight, Melman.
Go to *sleep* already, Melman!
Herrr...
Snark...
Alex, what in the black and white blazes is the matter with you? **Go to sleep!**

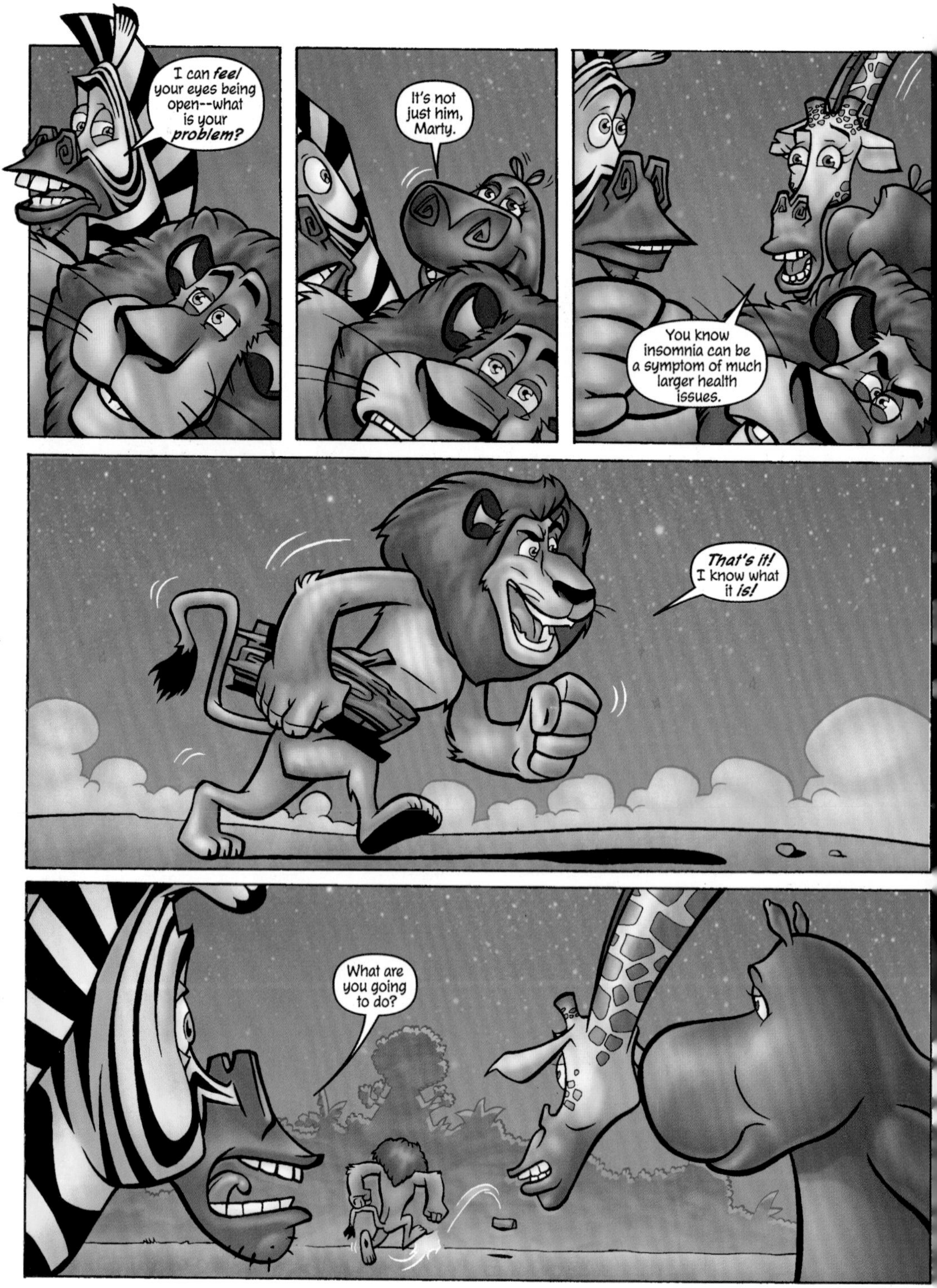
I can *feel* your eyes being open--what is your ***problem?***
It's not just him, Marty.
You know insomnia can be a symptom of much larger health issues.
That's it! I know what it *is!*
What are you going to do?

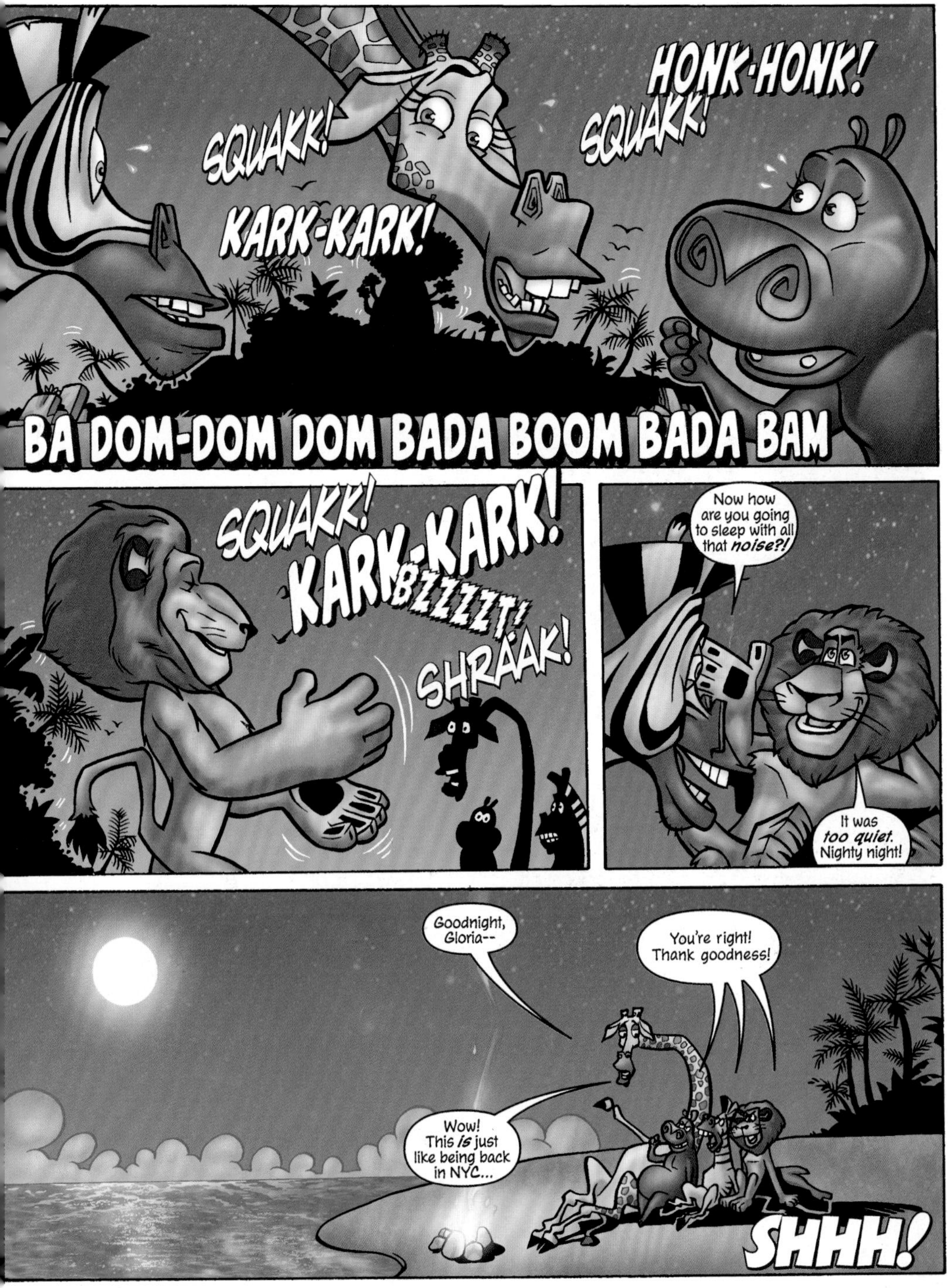

SQUAKK!
KARK-KARK!
HONK-HONK!
SQUAKK!
BA DOM-DOM DOM BADA BOOM BADA BAM
SQUAKK!
KARK-KARK!
BZZZZT!
SHRAAK!
Now how are you going to sleep with all that *noise?!*
It was *too quiet.* Nighty night!
Goodnight, Gloria--
You're right! Thank goodness!
Wow! This *is* just like being back in NYC...
SHHH!

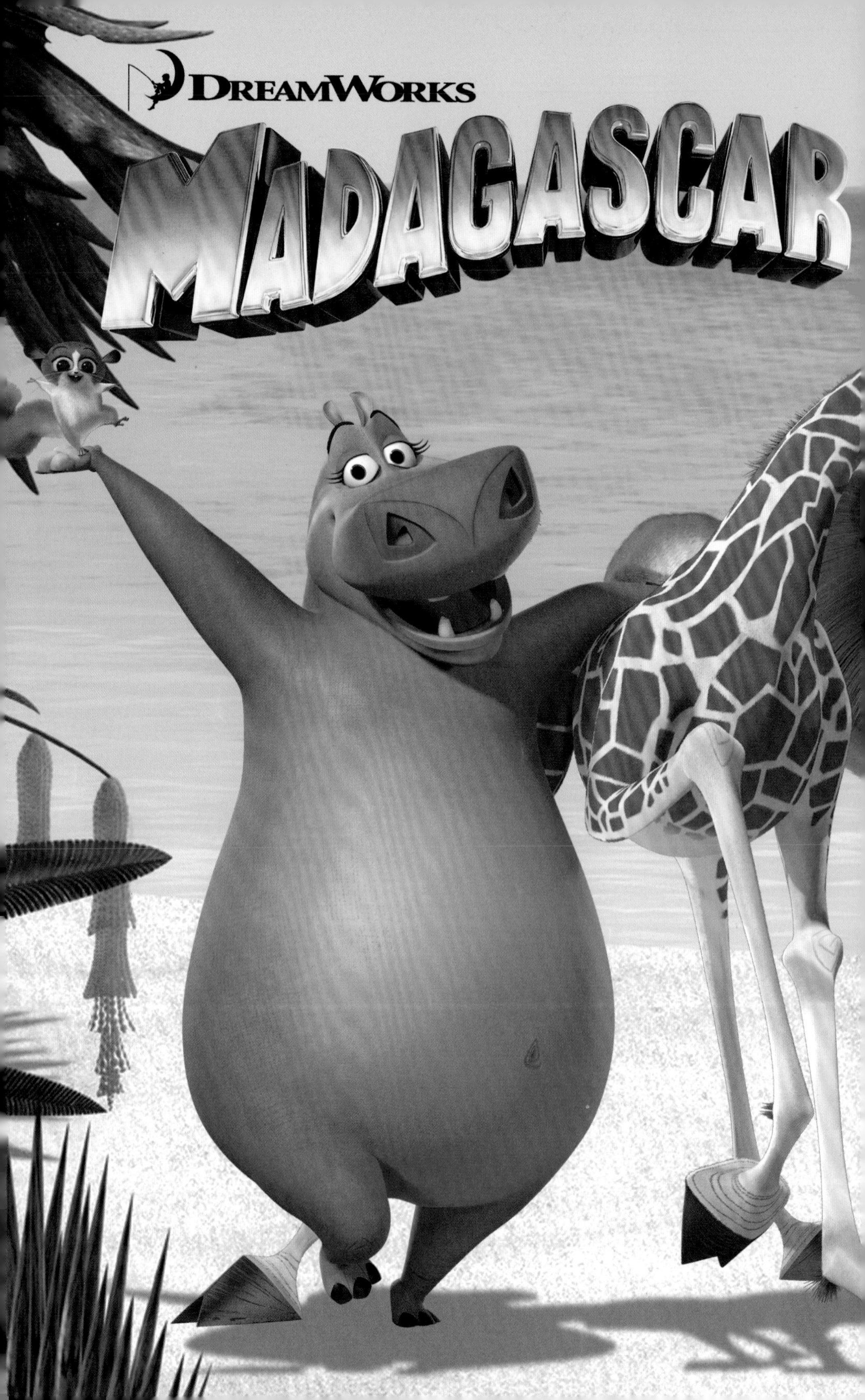
DREAMWORKS
MADAGASCAR

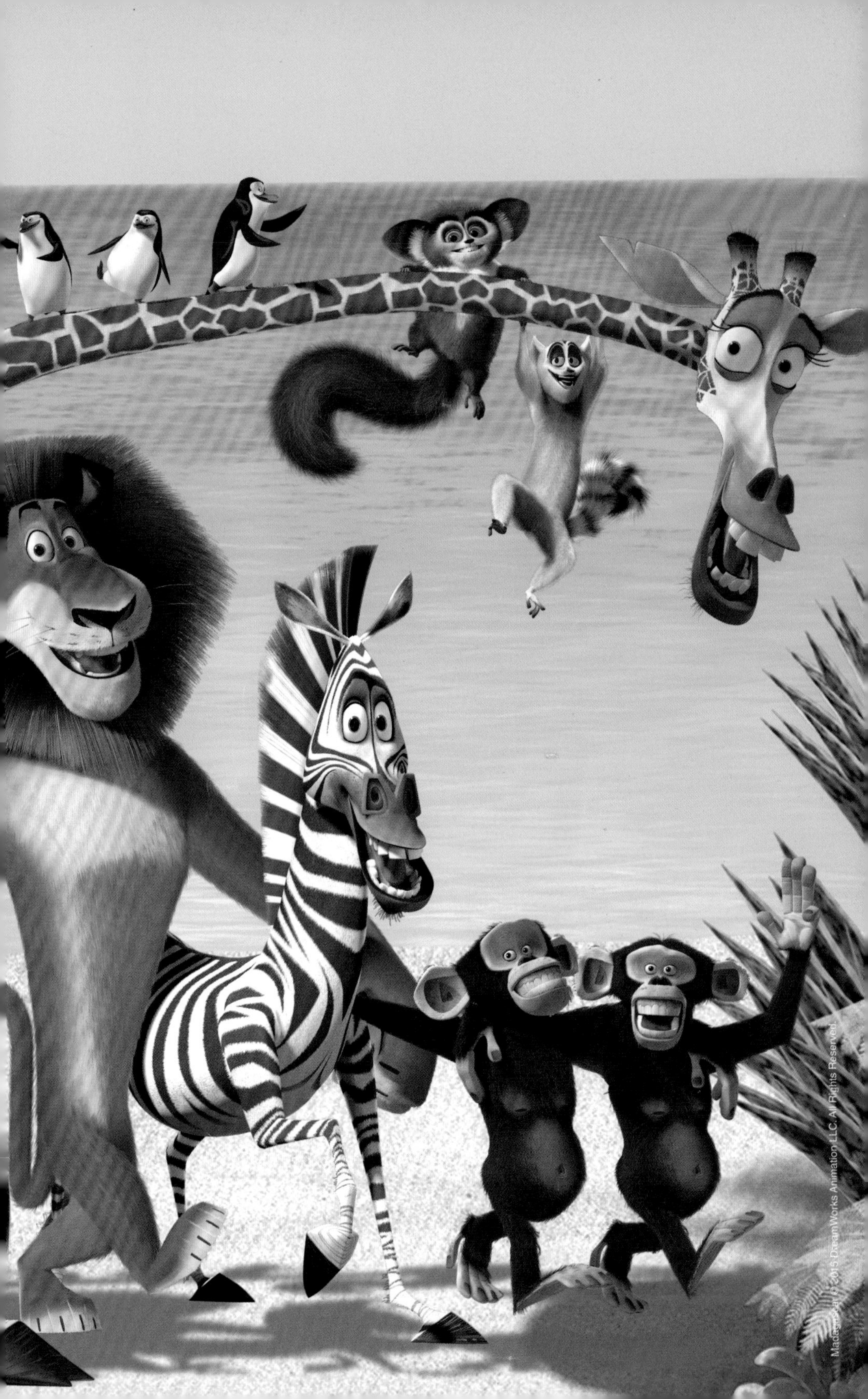

HOUSE HASSLES

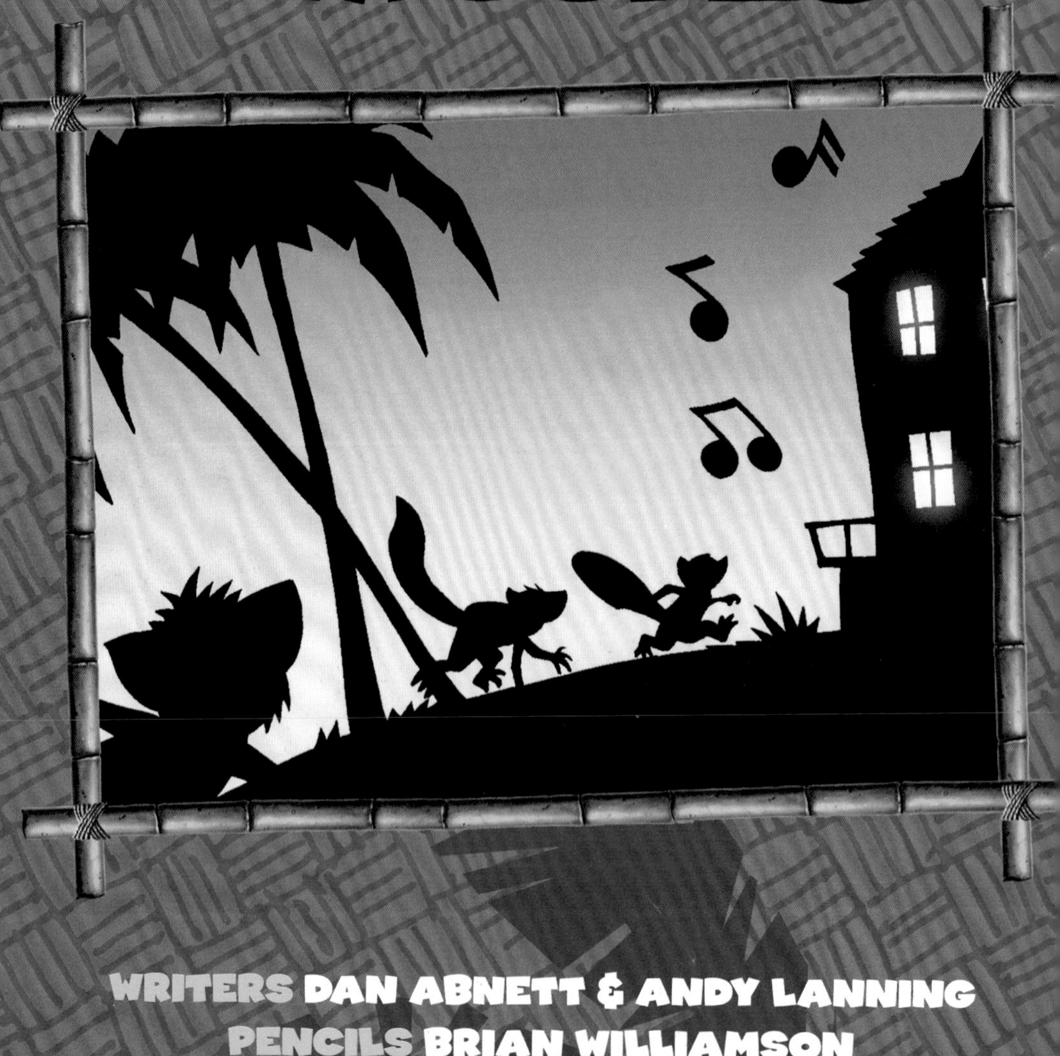

WRITERS DAN ABNETT & ANDY LANNING
PENCILS BRIAN WILLIAMSON
INKS BAMBOS GEORGIOU
COLORS WILDIDEAS
LETTERS JIMMY BETANCOURT/COMICRAFT

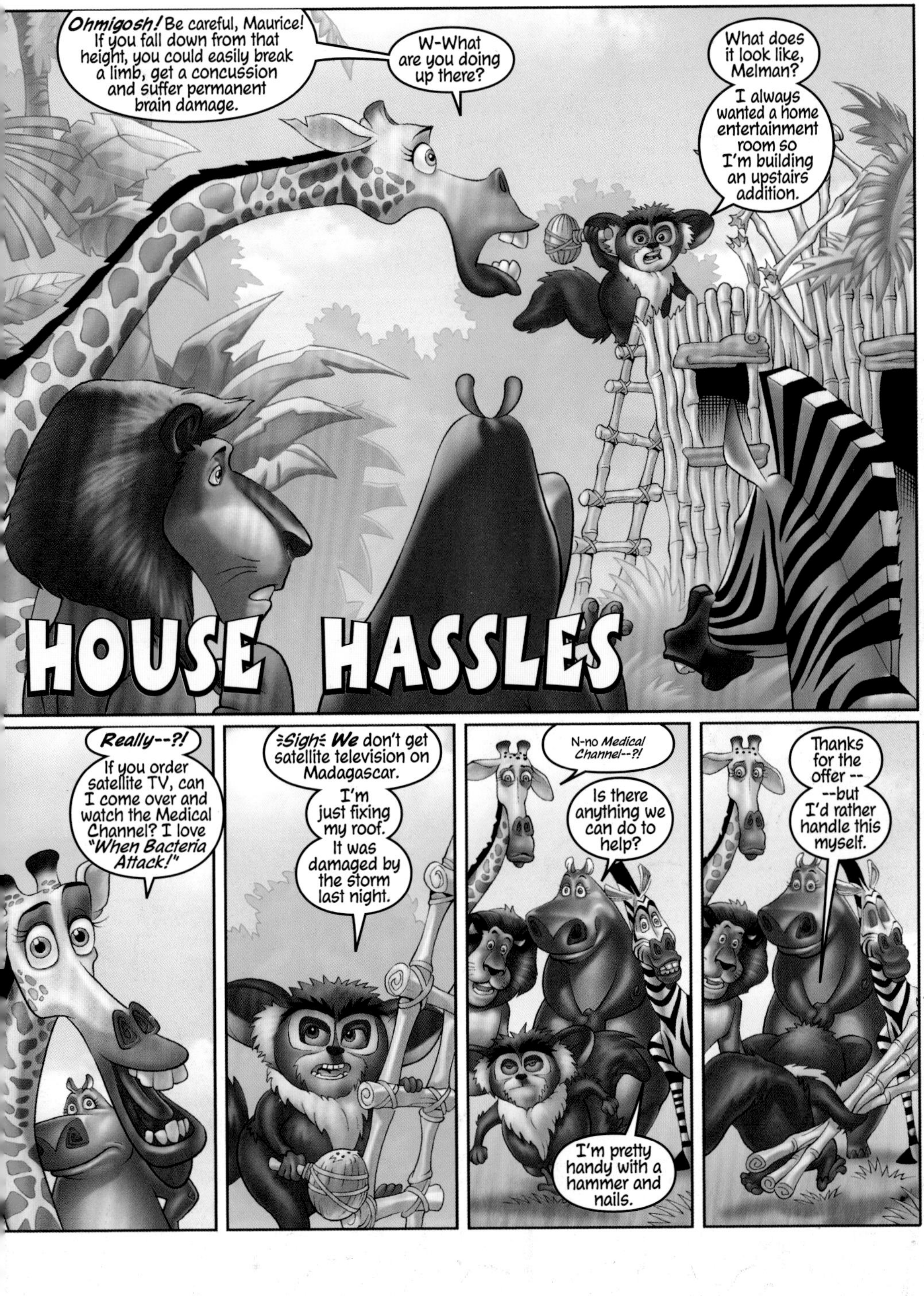

Ohmigosh! Be careful, Maurice! If you fall down from that height, you could easily break a limb, get a concussion and suffer permanent brain damage.
W-What are you doing up there?
What does it look like, Melman?
I always wanted a home entertainment room so I'm building an upstairs addition.
HOUSE HASSLES
Really--?!
If you order satellite TV, can I come over and watch the Medical Channel? I love "When Bacteria Attack!"
Sigh We don't get satellite television on Madagascar.
I'm just fixing my roof.
It was damaged by the storm last night.
N-no Medical Channel--?!
Is there anything we can do to help?
I'm pretty handy with a hammer and nails.
Thanks for the offer --
--but I'd rather handle this myself.

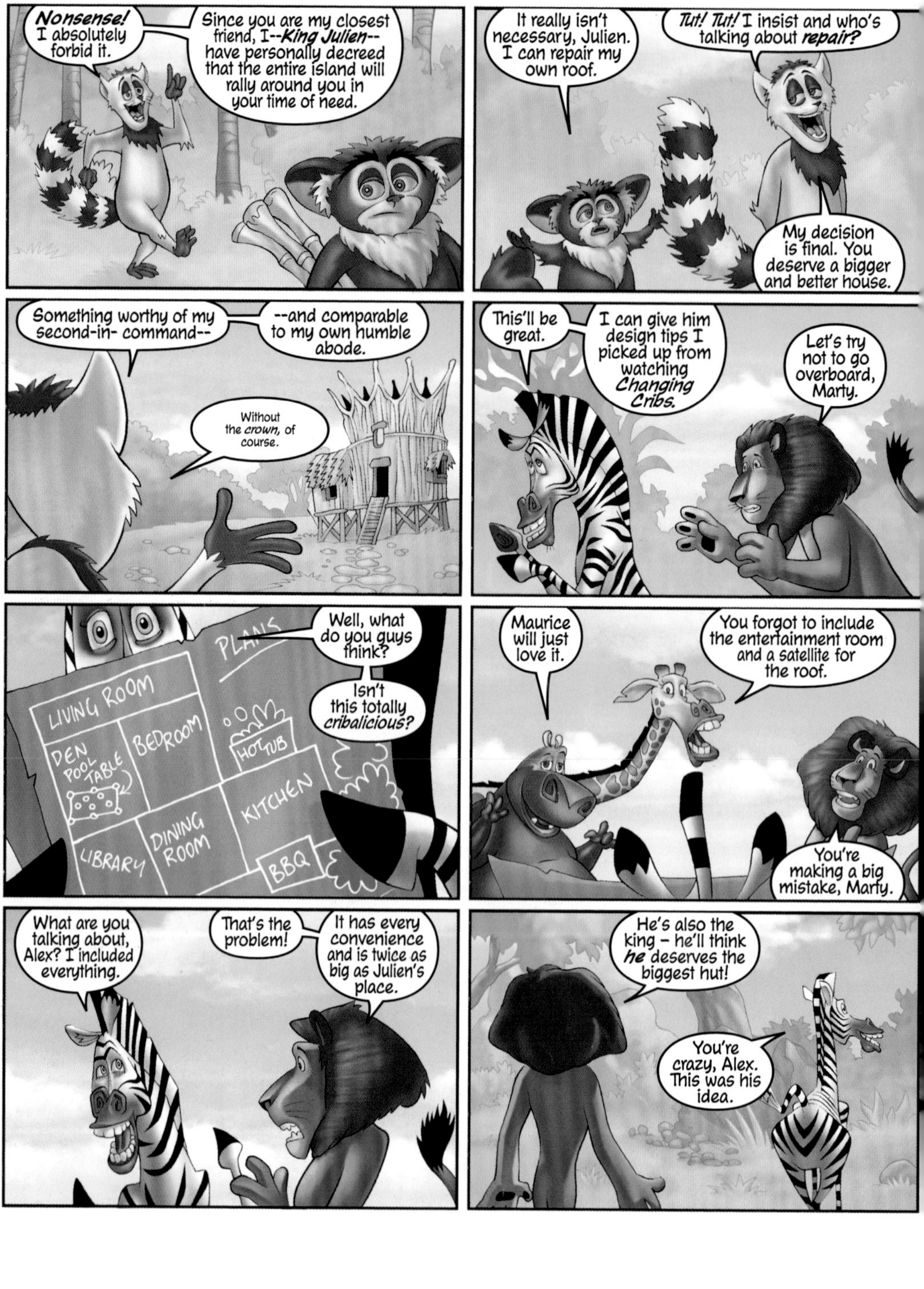
Nonsense! I absolutely forbid it.
Since you are my closest friend, I--King Julien--have personally decreed that the entire island will rally around you in your time of need.
It really isn't necessary, Julien. I can repair my own roof.
Tut! Tut! I insist and who's talking about repair?
My decision is final. You deserve a bigger and better house.
Something worthy of my second-in- command--
--and comparable to my own humble abode.
Without the crown, of course.
This'll be great.
I can give him design tips I picked up from watching Changing Cribs.
Let's try not to go overboard, Marty.
PLANS
LIVING ROOM
BEDROOM
DEN
POOL TABLE
HOT TUB
KITCHEN
DINING ROOM
LIBRARY
BBQ
Well, what do you guys think?
Isn't this totally cribalicious?
Maurice will just love it.
You forgot to include the entertainment room and a satellite for the roof.
You're making a big mistake, Marty.
What are you talking about, Alex? I included everything.
That's the problem!
It has every convenience and is twice as big as Julien's place.
He's also the king – he'll think he deserves the biggest hut!
You're crazy, Alex. This was his idea.

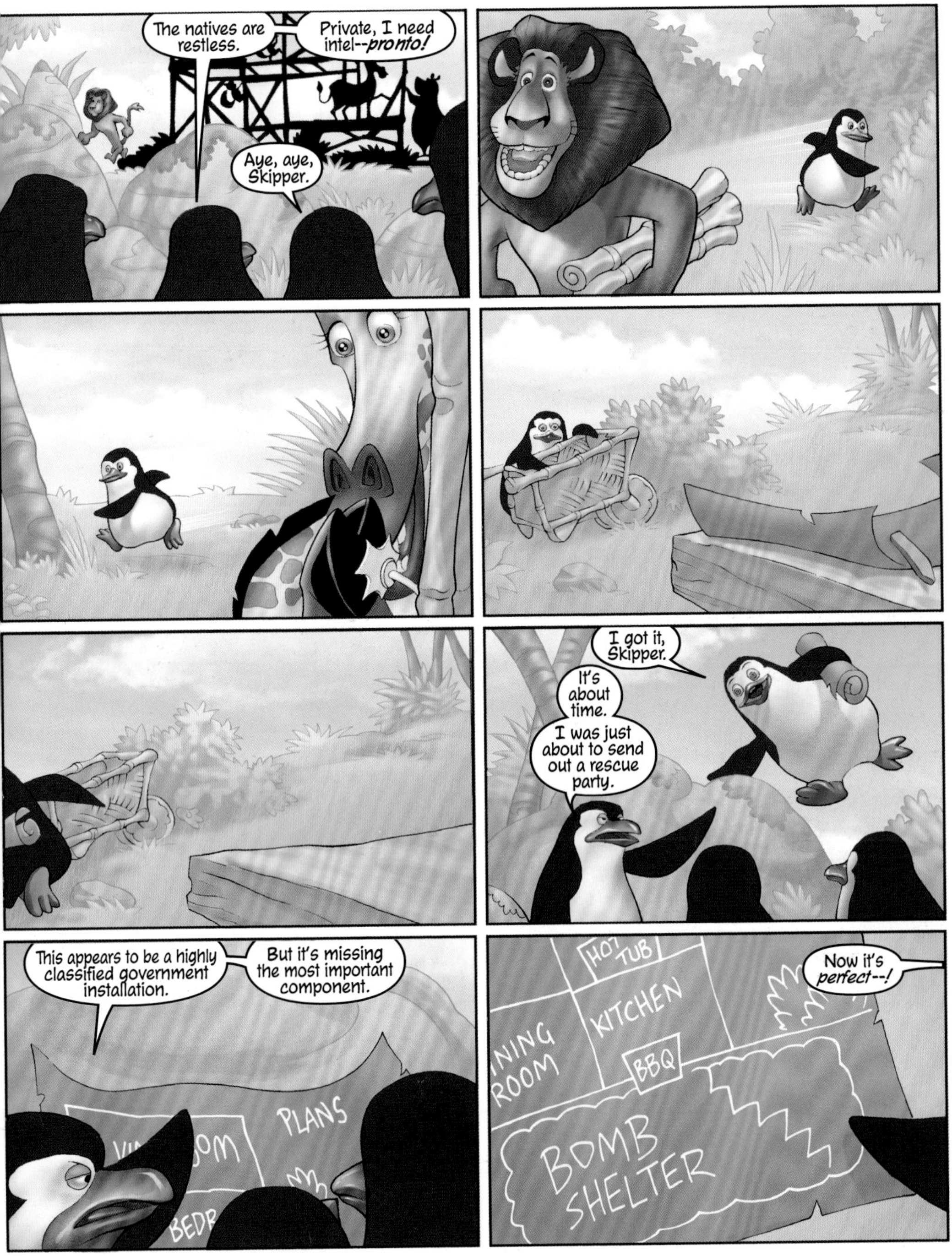
The natives are restless.
Private, I need intel--*pronto!*
Aye, aye, Skipper.
I got it, Skipper.
It's about time.
I was just about to send out a rescue party.
This appears to be a highly classified government installation.
But it's missing the most important component.
PLANS
HOT TUB
KITCHEN
BBQ
BOMB SHELTER
Now it's *perfect--!*

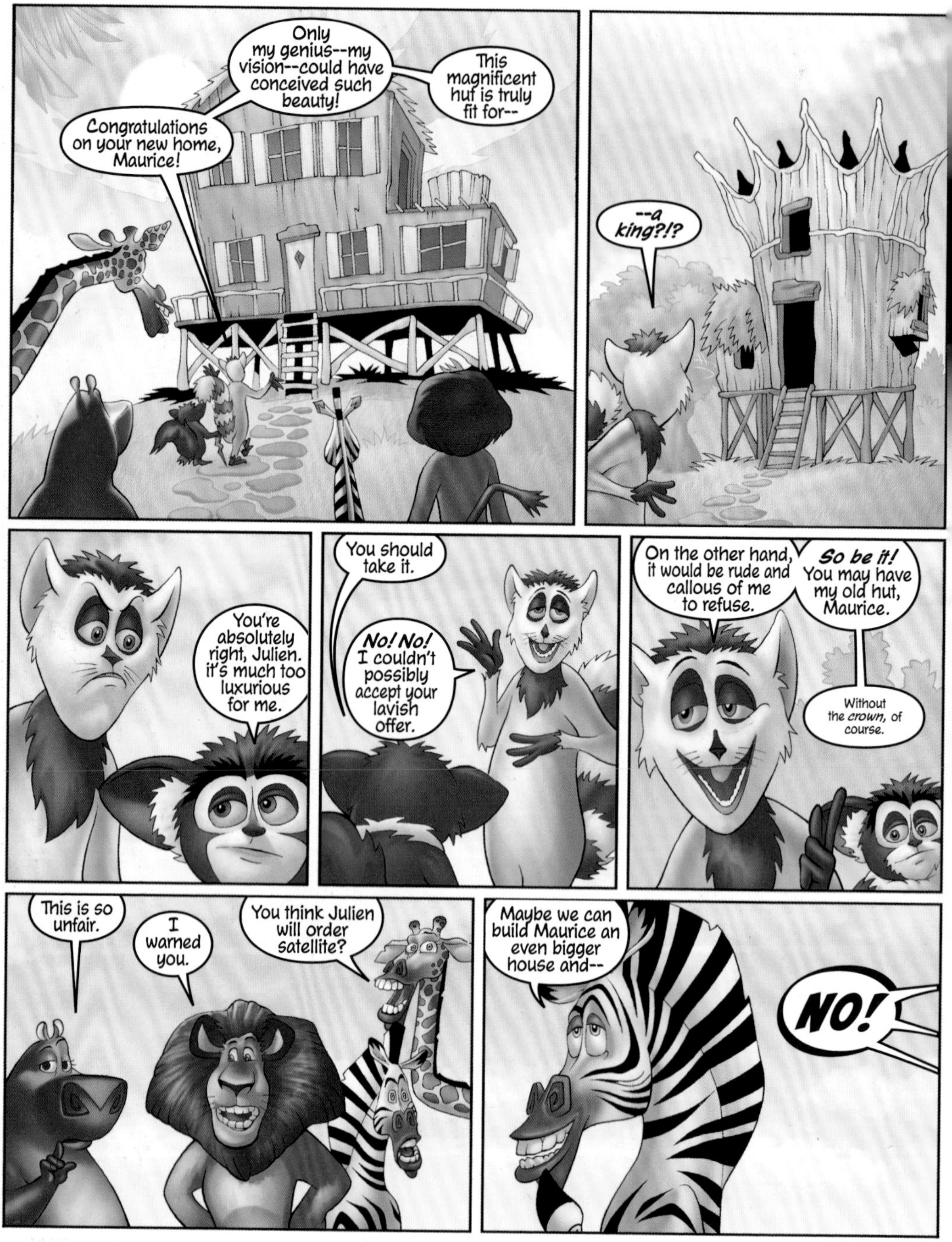
Congratulations on your new home, Maurice!
Only my genius--my vision--could have conceived such beauty!
This magnificent hut is truly fit for--
--a king?!?
You're absolutely right, Julien. it's much too luxurious for me.
You should take it.
No! No! I couldn't possibly accept your lavish offer.
On the other hand, it would be rude and callous of me to refuse.
So be it! You may have my old hut, Maurice.
Without the crown, of course.
This is so unfair.
I warned you.
You think Julien will order satellite?
Maybe we can build Maurice an even bigger house and--
NO!

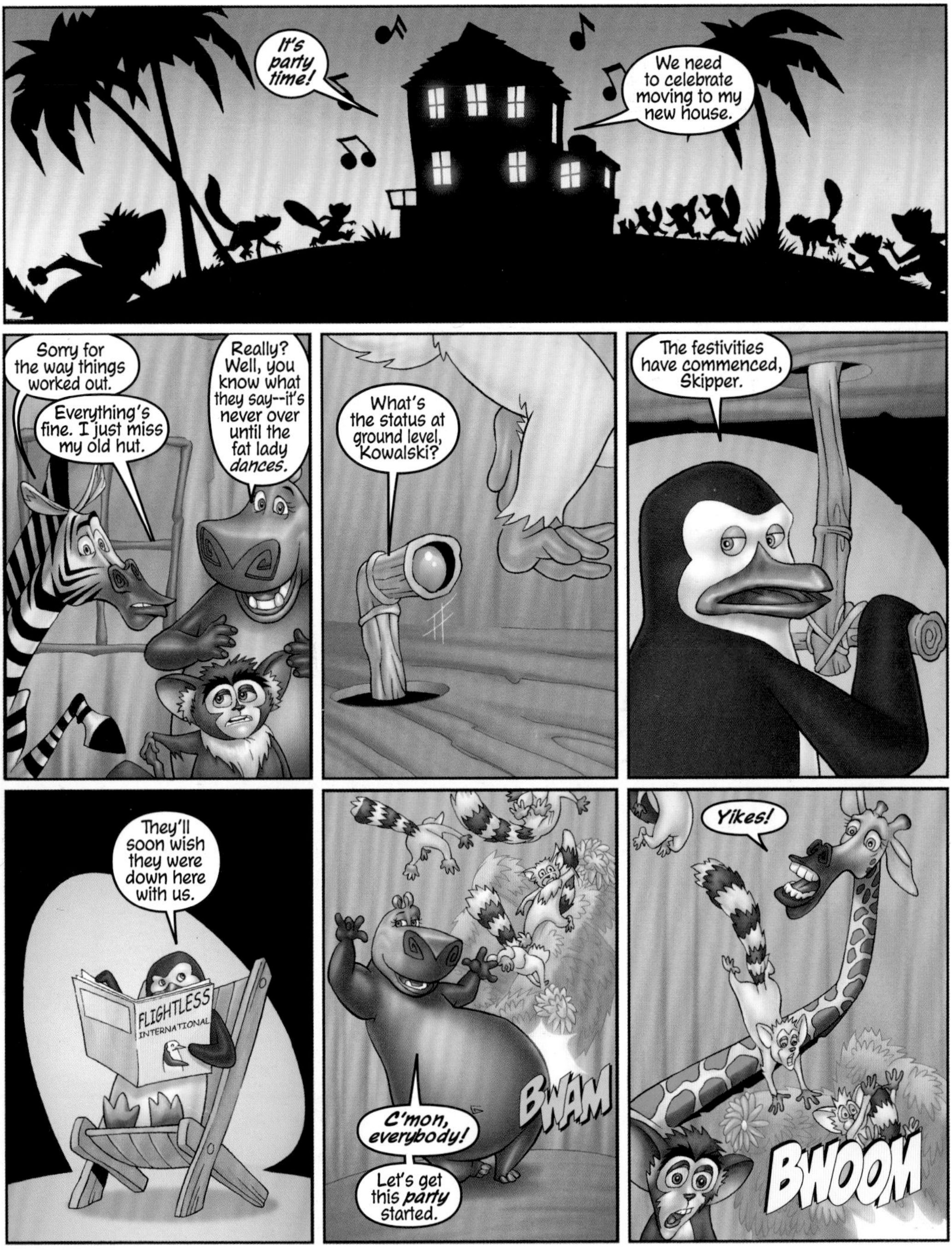
It's party time!
We need to celebrate moving to my new house.
Sorry for the way things worked out.
Everything's fine. I just miss my old hut.
Really? Well, you know what they say--it's never over until the fat lady dances.
What's the status at ground level, Kowalski?
The festivities have commenced, Skipper.
They'll soon wish they were down here with us.
FLIGHTLESS INTERNATIONAL
BWAM
C'mon, everybody!
Let's get this party started.
Yikes!
BWOOM

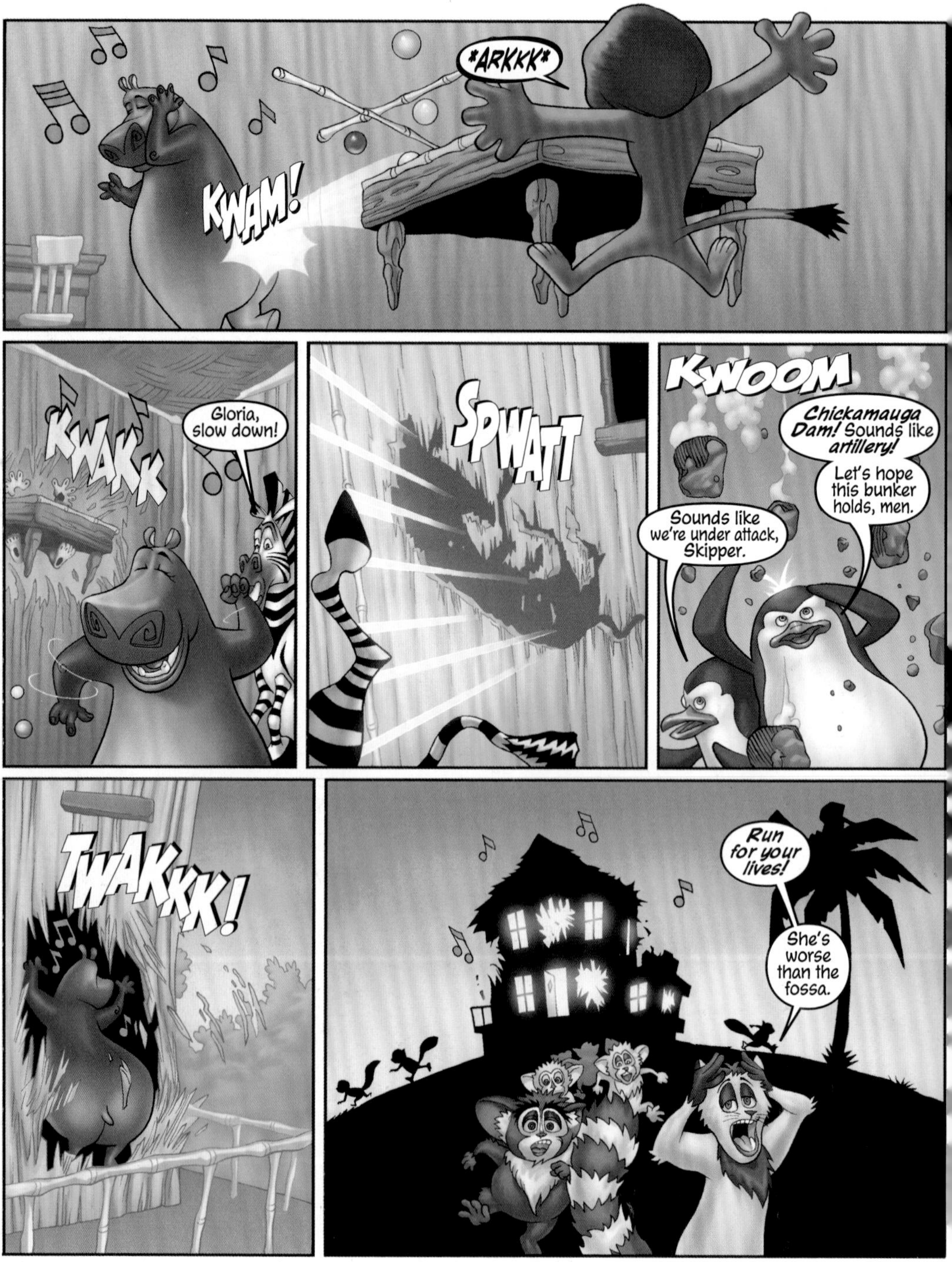

ARKKK
KWAM!
KWAKK
Gloria, slow down!
SPWATT
KWOOM
Chickamauga Dam! Sounds like artillery!
Let's hope this bunker holds, men.
Sounds like we're under attack, Skipper.
TWAKKK!
Run for your lives!
She's worse than the fossa.

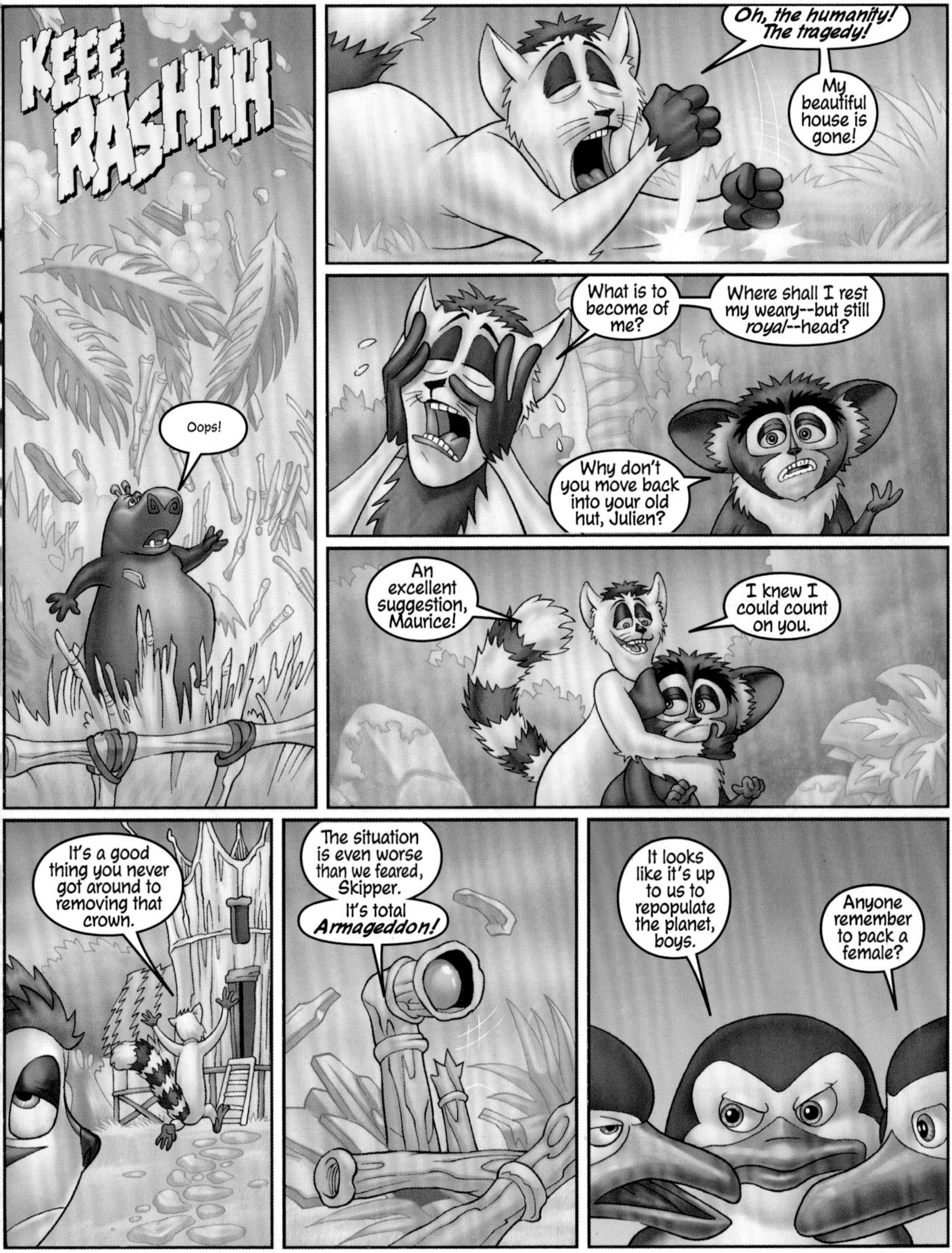
KEEE RASHHH
Oops!
Oh, the humanity! The tragedy!
My beautiful house is gone!
What is to become of me?
Where shall I rest my weary--but still *royal*--head?
Why don't you move back into your old hut, Julien?
An excellent suggestion, Maurice!
I knew I could count on you.
It's a good thing you never got around to removing that crown.
The situation is even worse than we feared, Skipper.
It's total *Armageddon!*
It looks like it's up to us to repopulate the planet, boys.
Anyone remember to pack a female?

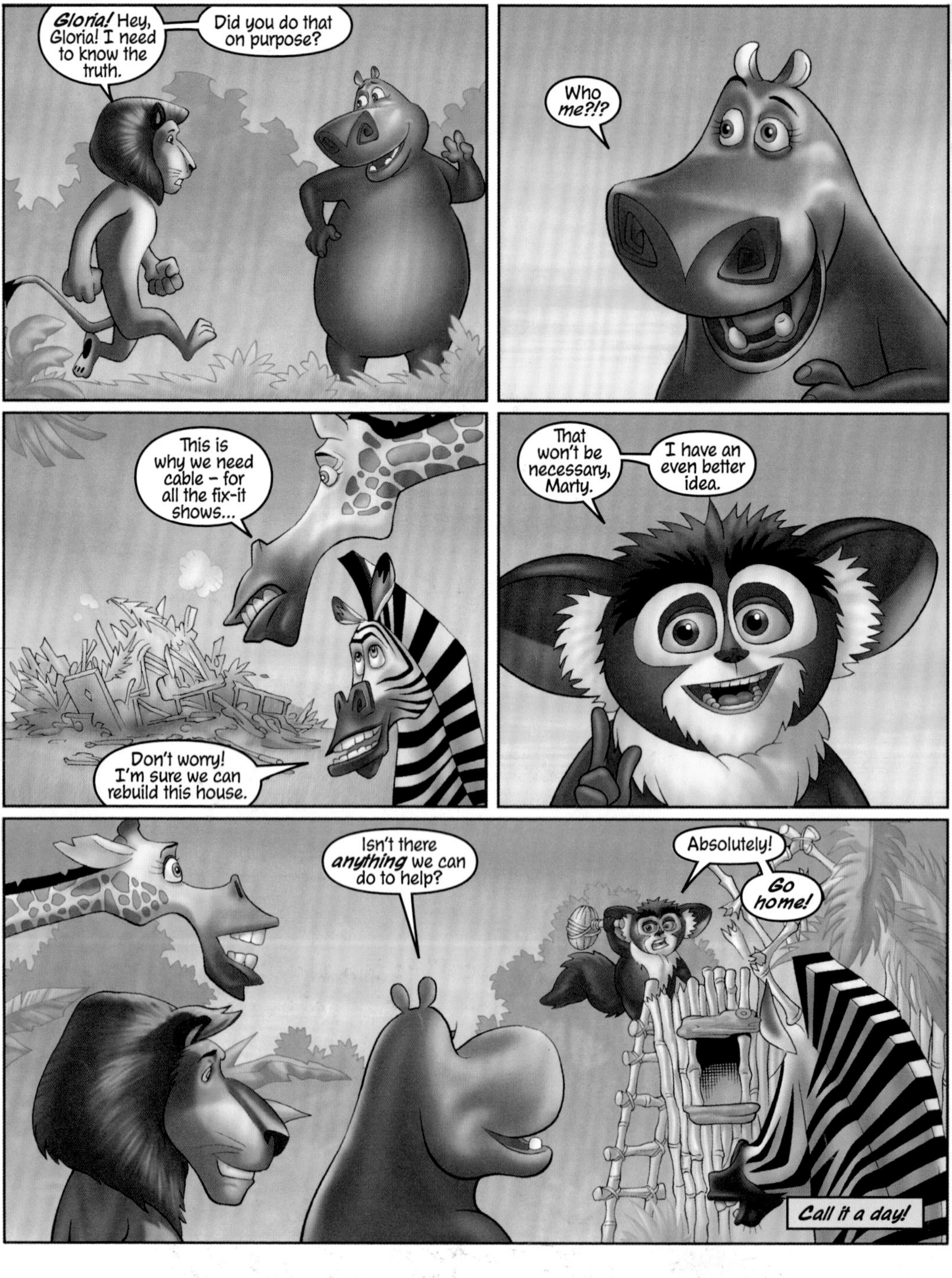
Gloria! Hey, Gloria! I need to know the truth.
Did you do that on purpose?
Who me?!?
This is why we need cable – for all the fix-it shows...
Don't worry! I'm sure we can rebuild this house.
That won't be necessary, Marty.
I have an even better idea.
Isn't there anything we can do to help?
Absolutely!
Go home!
Call it a day!

HOME VOL. 1

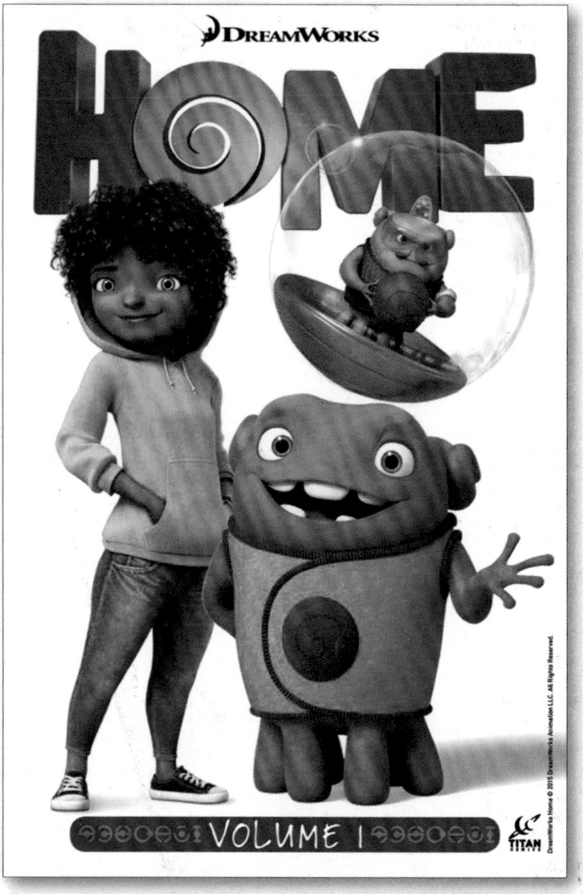
DREAMWORKS
HOME
VOLUME 1
TITAN

BRAND NEW STORIES FEATURING OH, TIP, PIG AND THE BOOV FROM DREAMWORKS ANIMATION'S SMASH HIT MOVIE, *HOME!*

Based on DreamWorks Animation's smash hit movie *Home*, Titan Comics bring you the all-new adventures of the friendliest, goofiest world dominators you've ever seen!

In these original stories, Tip and the Boov alien, Oh, attempt to play hide-and-seek – with inter-dimensional consequences! And Oh faces the perilous pitfalls of job-hunting! Plus, 'Pig in Space' and 'The Funny Pages'!

ON SALE NOW!
WWW.TITAN-COMICS.COM

TITAN COMICS

DREAMWORKS ANIMATION SKG

DREAMWORKS DRAGONS: RIDERS OF BERK

Titan Comics presents the most exciting *DreamWorks Dragons: Riders of Berk* adventure yet, written by Simon Furman (*Transformers, Matt Hatter Chronicles*) with incredible art by rising star Iwan Nazif!

During a routine training exercise, Hiccup and his friends discover a huge, mysterious cave in a forest near Berk... meanwhile, Stoick investigates the disappearance of a number of fishing vessels and bumps into an old enemy!

VOLUME 6 ON SALE NOW!
WWW.TITAN-COMICS.COM

PENGUINS OF MADAGASCAR GRAPHIC NOVEL COLLECTION

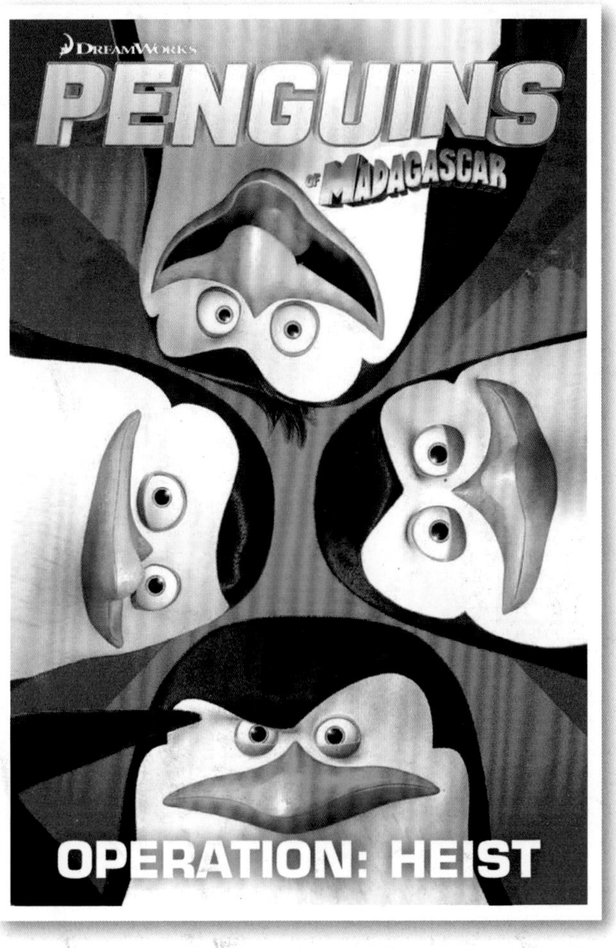
DreamWorks
PENGUINS
OF MADAGASCAR
OPERATION: HEIST

AWESOME COMIC STRIP ANTICS FROM THE PENGUINS OF MADAGASCAR!

You've seen them in their own brilliant movie, now read their hilarious comic strips in this brand new collection. In 'Big Top,' the penguins' circus gets a new recruit – the mysterious Claude the Clown... And then in 'Operation: Heist,' arch-villain Clepto the Magpie is on the loose, and he brainwashes Rico into doing his dirty work!

VOLUME 2 ON SALE NOW!

WWW.TITAN-COMICS.COM

TITAN COMICS

DreamWorks ANIMATION SKG

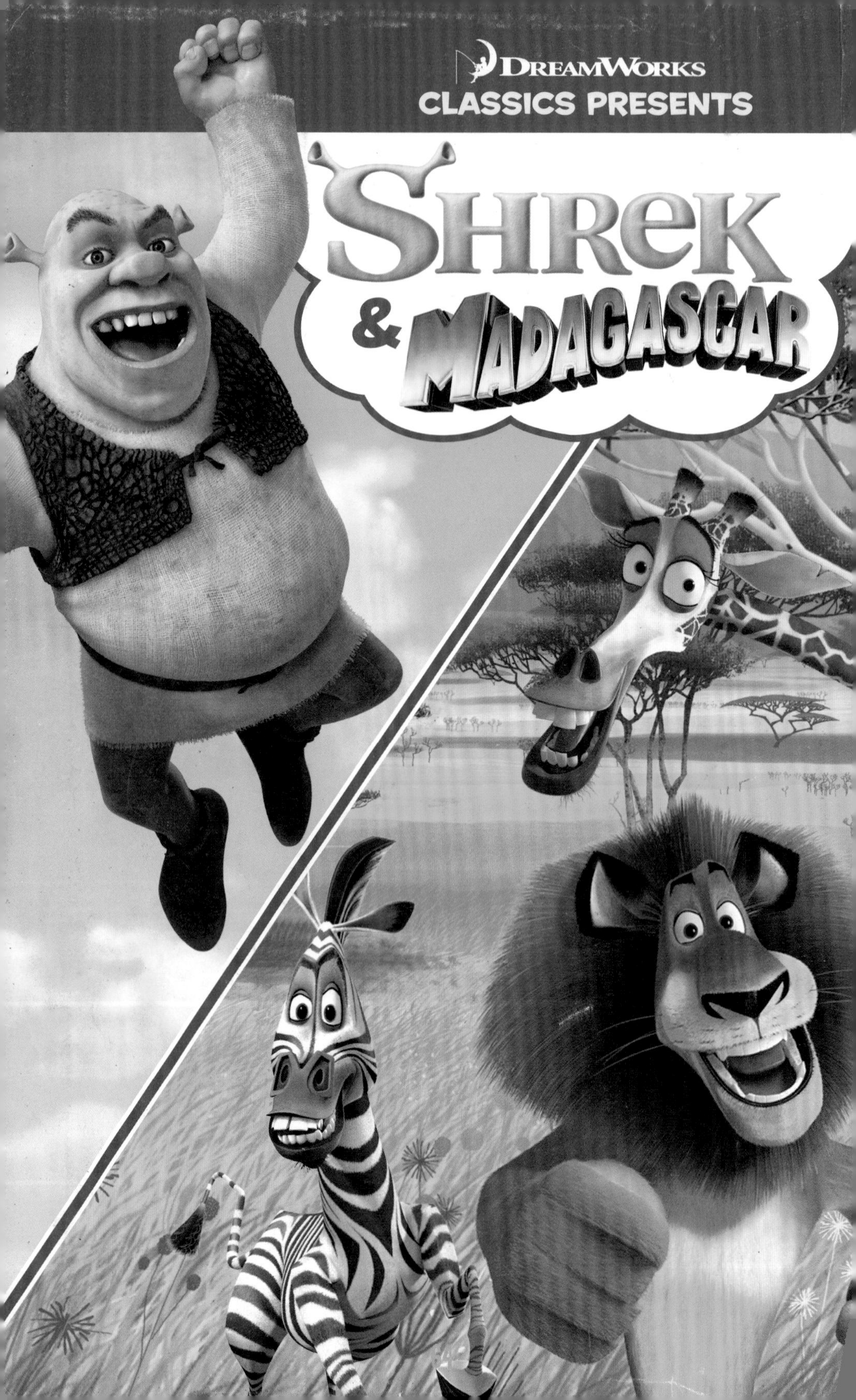
DreamWorks
CLASSICS PRESENTS
Shrek
& Madagascar